# A Philosopher Adrift in the Sea of Time

By

Michael Baum

# Previous publications

**Fiction**

The Third Tablet of the Holy Covenant
Aaron's Rod
The Nile Delta mystery
The Class of 1960

**Non-Fiction**

Breast Beating
The Scepticaemic Surgeon
The History & Mystery of Breast Cancer
Why am I a Jew? - Spinoza revisited

# Contents

# Chapter 1

Friday Night with the Tannenbaum's, May 2023

Jonathan Tannenbaum was celebrating his eighty-third birthday, his second bar mitzvah; three score years and ten plus thirteen. It coincided with the date of his retirement from the chair of the history and philosophy of science at the London School of Economics thirteen years in the past. He had been a protégée of Karl Popper and shared his views on the practical aspects of conjectures and refutations. Where he differed from his mentor was at the boundaries of rationalism and metaphysics. In other words, he didn't share Popper's dogma that *falsifiability* was the touchstone of epistemology.

He was a happy man who could look backwards at a very successful career and an equally successful marriage to his beautiful and exotic wife, Shoshana, who had a doctorate in neurophysiology. They had three children, a son and two daughters, who had married within the faith. Richard, a consultant surgeon at the Royal Free Hospital. Rachel, who married a hedge fund trader, was exceptionally wealthy with a house with one set of stairs running up and another set of stairs running down, in Hampstead Garden Suburb. They also owned a "cottage" with seven bedrooms and a swimming pool, in the Cotswolds. His youngest, Helen, married a modern orthodox rabbi in Stanmore who lived in a modest house provided by the community together with a modest stipend.

He was also looking forward to the near future when his granddaughter; Luna, first born of Rachel, would marry one of his ex-students, Avram Saadeh, who like his wife was born in Jerusalem. As well as one granddaughter, his three very successful children had delivered him with eight grandsons, all of whom loved and respected their grandfather but none of whom had elected to study philosophy. They were all at universities or colleges studying a broad spectrum of subjects that included engineering, Adam; computer science, Joshua; the history of art; Leo; drama, Sam; psychology, Zack; geography, David; popular music, Joe; and the youngest, Benjamin, son of Helen, studying in a *yeshiva*. All of them were fanatical supporters of football clubs that included Arsenal, Spurs, QPR and Crystal Palace.

Football was of no interest to their grandfather but their in-house disputes and the passion of their loyalty to the club of their choice, hatched a philosophical conundrum in this old man's head for an explanation for these tribal loyalties.

It was one of those Friday night dinners when the whole family gathered to feast after lighting the Sabbath Candles and blessing the wine and chola bread. That Friday night was not only the eve of *Shabbat* but also the eve of Jonathan's second bar mitzvah. As well as the traditional dinner they were enjoying the traditional good-natured discussion of the chances of Arsenal versus Spurs the following day whilst in parallel explaining to each other how to achieve peace in the Middle East. Amongst the boys on this topic, there were two opinions, the politically right wing who happened to be the Arsenal supporters and the politically left wingers who happened to support the Spurs. The debate got louder and louder like an arms race and there was also some confusion between the two topics, as right and left wingers also could be interpreted as the football players who kicked the ball down the right or left strip of the pitch. Once the din reached eighty decibels, their grandfather couldn't take any more and banged the table with the appropriate stainless-steel instrument called a tablespoon, a multi-purpose device that had just been used for drinking chicken soup.

"Boys, boys, *shekket, shekket,* you are giving me a headache. As it's my bar mitzvah I want a degree of decorum and out of respect allow me to direct the conversation in a structured way." To his amazement, there was a sudden silence in the room, an event so alarming that his wife and two daughters who were sorting out the portions of roast chicken and roasted potatoes in the kitchen, came running in to see what disaster had befallen the family.

Once the natural background noise of the dining room was restored, Jonathan began a monologue to explain an enigma that was bothering him for years that would make a more appropriate theme for a discussion at the feast that welcomed in the Sabbath on the eve of his second bar mitzva.

"My dear wife, children, grandchildren, daughter-in-law, sons-in-law and Avram, soon to be a full member of my extended family, lend me your ears. Shoshana thinks I talk too much and can be boring, she may be right but allow me to beg your tolerance on this special occasion.

Let me start with a well-known paradox. If a tree, let's say a fir tree, falls in a forest and there is no one there, does it make a noise?"

All the grandchildren responded in unison but in the din, it was impossible to hear, so their grandfather called for order and asked Adam, the oldest of the grandchildren to respond. "Grandpa, you taught us the answer to this when we were in primary school. The answer is no. To make a noise you must have a sound source and a sound receiver. Sound waves are generated as the tree hits the ground, but noise can only be received if there is an ear drum nearby to pick up the sound waves."

"Very good answer Adam, I'm glad you have learnt something from me, but the next question is more complex. If there is no one near enough to hear the tree fall that means no one can see the tree so, how can we say that such a tree exists?"

Benjamin, the youngest then responded, "Well that's easy. A plane might be flying overhead, and the pilot looks down."

"That's a smart response, although he can't see the specific tree in a forest. By the way, in case you've forgotten, Tannenbaum is German for fir tree and as you may have predicted where this roundtable chat is leading – family trees not coniferous trees. But you are right, Benjamin, a pilot is a member of the homo sapiens, so for trees or any other inanimate object to exist you need the sensory organs of one of our species."

Adam responded immediately, "Grandpa, I bear the name of the first man created by Hashem but in spite of all of us having rejected creationism, there must have been an evolutionary period of thousands of years during which time primates like the chimpanzee, reached a point of awareness of inanimate objects that would provide food. They might not eat cones, but they must surely have learnt to distinguish banana trees from coconut trees." "*Kol ha'kavoed,* all honour to you for that elegant response, but what happens when that chimpanzee dies?" All grandsons, and one granddaughter replied in unison, "There are hundreds of other monkeys."

"Indeed" he replied, "but think for a moment, *He,* the pronoun is used to identify one man from amongst the many-the singular human differentiated from the many, with a will of his own and a unique personality, was a perception which must have come late in human development. Scientists believe that this power of – what are we calling it – awareness is that which separates humans from animals. But if this is a faculty of the mind which evolves as the human reason has evolved, or our ability to make things, then we are only animals after all. Or perhaps awareness is a thing which is there but which we do not yet completely see or use, as for many millions of years human beings did not have fire, or electricity. These are rhetorical questions that lead me on to contemplate family trees.

Now forgive me if I drift into a metaphysical way of thinking. I believe that our earth has a fourth stratum in addition to the oceans, the earth, and the atmosphere; this stratum I would call the sea of human consciousness. This remarkable sea covers most of the landmasses of the earth and its ripples vary in height above the ground. This sea of consciousness is of course contained somewhere in the cerebral cortex of several billion members of the species homo sapiens, and it is a strange sea because on closer examination it is made up of quanta of energy bobbing about inside strange fruit from strange trees. These trees have very old roots anchored to the time when man first lost his innocence in the Garden of Eden and recognised that his life was like a passing shadow. This strange fruit, as I call them, are released from the tree at birth but defy the law of gravity and float upward because of the property of buoyancy within this strange sea of human consciousness. As time goes on this property weakens and eventually all buoyancy is lost and the fruit falls. This fallen fruit is more than compensated by new orbs of living consciousness; and as fruit never fall too far from their tree, these newcomers will share and perpetuate the genetic code of their forbears, although with ever-increasing dilution. It is my fondest wish that when I die my beloved grandchildren will bring forth into this sea of my imagination children who will all be one eighth me and one eighth *safta,* Shoshana."

At this point, Shoshana joined in. "Forgive me contradicting you, Johnathan, our children will also inherit qualities from us that are independent of the genetic code. I agree that inheritance is typically associated with the Mendelian transmission of information from parents to offspring by DNA sequences known as genes. However, empirical data clearly suggest that traits can be acquired from ancestors by mechanisms that do not involve genetic alleles, referred to as non-genetic inheritance. Information that is non-genetically transmitted across generations includes parental experience and exposure to certain environments, but also parental mutations, because they can change the parental 'intrinsic' environment. Non-genetic inheritance is not limited to the first generation of the progeny but can involve the grandchildren and even further generations. My particular interest in my research is the inheritance of behavioural abnormalities pertinent to psychiatric disorders. Multigenerational non-genetic inheritance is often interpreted as the transmission of epigenetic marks, such as DNA methylation, via the egg or sperm. However, information can be carried across generations by many bioactive substances, including hormones, cytokines, and even microorganisms, without the involvement of the eggs and sperms. We reason that this broader definition of non-genetic inheritance is more appropriate, especially in the context of psychiatric disorders, because of the well-recognised role of parental and early life environmental factors in later life psychopathology."

At this point, Joshua piped up. "Grandma, you know my interest in artificial intelligence, if I understand you correctly, your memories as well as your intelligence can be inherited by me."

"Now you mention it, Josh, I think you might be right. Since the 1960s, more than 2,000 children from across the world have described apparent recollections from a previous life, all documented in a database maintained by the Division of Perceptual Studies within the Department of Psychiatry and Neurobehavioral Sciences at the University of Virginia School of Medicine. Sometimes a child presents enough identifying information for relatives or researchers to pinpoint a deceased person."

Zack the psychologist then joined in, "Might that account for my bouts of *deja vu*?"

"Great idea, Zack, but *deja vu* always give you a sense of having been or done something like this in the past." "Not necessarily, Grandma, sometimes they suggest other peoples' memories!"

Then Joshua interrupted again, " I think the answer to all these questions is the number forty-two."

In unison the assembly shouted, "What?" "The number forty-two. In the novel by Douglas Adams, *The Hitchhiker's Guide to the Galaxy*, he concludes that the meaning of life, the universe, and everything, is forty-two, because that number is the answer given by a supercomputer, *Deep Thought*, with artificial intelligence that is a hundred times greater than that granted to Adam, who represents the first of the species, human sapiens. It sounds like a joke, but Douglas Adams was like me, a computer nerd and knew a lot about programming language. In programming an asterisk is translated to be 'whatever you want to be'. In ASCII language, the most basic computer software, forty-two is the designation for an asterisk. Deep Thought was asked what the true meaning of life was, and it answered, forty-two, 'anything you want it to be'. Grandpa is right in his definition of life being a strange sea of human consciousness, if that what he wants it to be, whereas for me forty-two means immersed in Grandma's chicken soup." Everyone fell about with laughter, and the roast chicken was served.

That night Jonathan had a nightmare that he arrived at the synagogue forgetting to dress himself, forgot the prayers before reading the haftorah, and went on the drop the scroll of the Torah when carrying it round back to the holy ark. He made nothing of this as he often expressed his subconscious anxiety in this manner.

# Chapter 2

## Highgate Synagogue the Following Morning

Jonathan's synagogue is in a modest modern building hiding down a narrow lane off the north road in Highgate village in northwest London. Yet it served its purpose more than most ostentatious synagogues he used to visit. The interior is panelled with polished wood of the colour burnt umber, interspersed with high stained-glass windows bearing the iconography of the high holy days. Women and men sit on the same level although at opposite sides of the sanctuary with an elaborate lace like ornamental metal *mechitza* that notionally preserves their modesty and protects the men from distraction when praying to the almighty. This in no way hides the fashionable hats the women wear on *Rosh Hashana,* the Jewish New Year, or the exchange of semaphore for silent conversations at a distance. He feels comfortably at home here and well-rehearsed for his chanting of the *haftarah* and *d'var ha Torah,* an exegesis of the passage of the day. After the reading of the law from the scroll of the *Sefer Torah* by the cantor, he was called up for the honour of reading the *haftarah* from the book of Joshua. It is said that all Jews are known by three names, in his case in English as Johnathan Tannenbaum, in the Hebrew name by which he was summoned to the *bimah, Yanatan Moishe ben Yitzhak,* and a third name only known to God for the righteous. His friends and his rabbi consider him righteous, and it was likely that Hashem shared this opinion. The *Parashas* for that day was *Shelach,* from *Barmidbar,* the book of numbers. This tells the tale of Moses sending out twelve spies to reconnoitre the land of Canaan, and he made this theme for his bar mitzvah sermon from the rabbi's lectern.

"My dear Rabbi, family and friends let me start my discourse with a blessing: *Blessed art thou, O Lord our God, king of the universe, who has kept us in life, and has preserved us, and enabled us to reach this time.* The life expectancy for a man in England and Wales currently is 78.6 years. I consider myself blessed for the additional 4.4 years I've been given to reach the age when I can celebrate my second bar mitzvah. I celebrated my first bar mitzvah in 1953 in the New Road Synagogue just off Whitechapel Road. We lived in Sydney Street in Stepney, a few doors down from the erstwhile anarchist's house made famous by the siege of Sydney Street in 1911, when Winston Churchill as home secretary took charge. Both my parents came from an orthodox Jewish background. My father, Isaac, was born in Warsaw and fled to this country in 1905 following the notorious pogrom when his parents were cut down by the marauding Cossacks, organised by supporters of the Romanov Czar as a distraction from the threat of a working-class uprising. How my father escaped from the imperial guards and arrived in Stepney as a lad of sixteen is an adventure story of its own; suffice it to say that it involved a perilous journey on foot and by horse and cart across Europe, along a network of Jewish communities until he reached Rotterdam. From there sailed to the port of London. He arrived as a penniless refugee fluent in Yiddish, Russian, and Ukrainian. As you can imagine I share enormous empathy for those migrants escaping Putin's war in Ukraine today. We were very poor, and my first bar mitzvah was more modest than we would expect these days. I did in fact have a fountain pen as a gift and a large Phaidon edition of the works of Leonardo da Vinci. That might explain my love for writing and fine art that I carry to this day. Let me now come to today's *parsha* that tells the story of the twelve spies Moses sent out into the land of Canaan and remind you of the first line of their report. 'We arrived at the land to which you sent us, and indeed it flows with milk and honey, and this is its fruit.' After the service is over you are all invited to a *kiddush* upstairs. Amongst the array of the usual delicatessen and Palwin number ten wine, you will note small glasses of an amber liquid that is a new Israeli whisky named 'Milk and Honey'. I promise you that it is superb and won a silver medal in a top tasting league. And yet it is young. After distillation it is matured in casks that had once carried kosher sherry. Those casks have been stored on the edge of the Dead Sea for only four years and yet it tastes better than any thirteen-year-old Speyside scotch. How can that be? Well, it's all to do with the atmosphere. The Milk and Honey fine malt comes of age in the Holy Land at four not thirteen years because of the heat and humidity at the lowest point on earth and now you will taste it at the highest point on earth. I look upon our synagogue, the epicentre of our community, as the highest point on earth. This honour is shared by all Jewish communities in the world. I look upon this synagogue as one of many casks of Milk and Honey, each leaving the sweet taste of sherry on the tongue. Our Milk and Honey also matures rapidly because of the atmosphere created by its membership and our beloved rabbi and Rebbetzin. I will finish my discourse with the words of Joshua ben Nun, the most optimistic of the spies; 'The land that we passed through was very good. If Hashem desires, he will bring us to this land. Do not rebel against the wishes of Hashem.' This land in my opinion has two meanings, the literal, *Erez Yisrael,* and figurative the sweet cask of our community." He sat down to the conventional cries from the male congregation: "*Shekoiach!*" After the service was over, they all traipsed upstairs to the big bright room used for celebrations and visiting lecturers, where food and drink were on display on seven circular tables. The rabbi chanted the *kiddush* and blessed the wine before the congregation were let loose on the buffet. At this point his rabbi came over to congratulate Jonathan on his bar mitzvah and on his sermon. The bar mitzvah "boy" in return thought his rabbi might be amused by the conversation he had with his family about the meaning of life the previous evening. To his surprise, Rabbi Cohen became animated. "Professor Tannenbaum, the number forty-two is considered holy in many ways amongst orthodox Jews and Kabbalists. It is said that God's name has forty-two letters, also forty-two is six times seven, six days representing the physical world and the seventh, Shabbat, the spiritual world. Furthermore, if *The Hitchhiker's Guide to the Galaxy*, concludes that forty-two also means the meaning of life is what you make of it, so does the Sedra, *Vaeschnan*. If the meaning of life is whatever you want, but life itself is the gift of God, then that means everything is encapsulated at this time, in this place enjoying a chat whilst drinking Milk and Honey. *L'chaim*."

***

That night Jonathan Tannenbaum sleep was disturbed by a recurring dream that he thought must have some occult meaning. He had read and enjoyed Sigmond Freud's masterpiece *The Interpretation of Dreams* but was sceptical of Freud's sexual symbolism. There was no scientific method to falsify these assertions, and all the beautiful narratives of his patient's dreams were interpreted to fit his prejudices, rather than data to build a fresh hypothesis.

Yet he expressed his genius with one sentence, "Every dream has at least one point where it eludes explanation – a sort of umbilicus linking it to the unknown." Jonathan's recurring dream was certainly classified in that category, very different to his dream of walking naked into his synagogue.

# Chapter 3

## Jonathan's Dream

This is how Jonathan described his dream to his wife, Shoshana, a neurophysiologist who worked alongside the psychiatrists at the nearby Tavistock clinic in Hampstead.

"My recurring dream starts when I'm leaving a large building that might be a hospital or a conference centre. I know that there are two exits from the building, one where I will always lose my way and the other where I'll know my way home. I always seem to choose the wrong way out and then start vacillating as to whether I came by car or not. I can't find my car, but I note the bright lights and busy road at the end of a lane where I'm sure to be able to use public transport to find my way home. When I get to the main road it's in bright sunlight but I've no idea where I'm standing. I then remember that I'm not in London but at a conference in another town at the same time I feel guilty that I've been away a week and never called you once. I bring out my mobile phone from my briefcase, but I can't make sense of the screen in a search for your number. I try to find a shop that deals with mobile phones without success and then suddenly remember I've a plane to catch to get back home. I try to order an Uber car to take me to the airport but again the phone lets me down as it's lost the app logo. I then remember I've left all my clothes in a chest of drawers back at the conference centre bedroom suites. I recall it has a grey door at the end of a long slanting corridor. I start running round in circles trying to find the narrow lane that leads back to the conference centre. At that point I wake up thanking the Lord it was all a dream."

"And that's also the point you wake me up screaming!" responded Shoshana.

"I'm so sorry, my darling, but I have to confess to you that I've started having panic attacks again. You remember when we had just got engaged and I was working for my PhD; I developed an anxiety-depressive illness. That started with panic attacks when I thought I was dying. The shrinks put me on some foul-tasting anti-depressives for about six months. But at least I had reasons for anxiety. I was working too hard and had financial problems worrying if we could afford a mortgage or even rent for an apartment close to our work. These days I consider myself one of the luckiest men alive. I have a wonderful wife, beloved children, and grandchildren, the mortgage has been paid off and we are looking forward to a summer holiday on the Amalfi coast."

"Well, I suppose your recurring dream might give us a clue to what's causing your panic attacks. I'm no expert in these matters but most of your dream is easy to interpret. You are wondering if you were in the wrong career all your life, you feel guilty about going off to so many conferences because of your fame, you once forgot to call me when you arrived safely in Japan about ten years ago, but I can only guess that the root of your problem is hidden behind the dark door at the end of the long corridor. You haven't been having an affair with that pretty young PhD student you're supervising, have you?" She ended with a laugh.

Before Jonathan had the chance to inhale enough air to refute that accusation, Shoshana put a finger on his lips and turning serious again, continued: "My darling husband, you are not gifted enough to keep secrets from me and I think you are far too old now to have an affair, if you are having panic attacks you need to see one of my colleagues at the Tavi. As you know traditional psychotherapy is long past its sell-by date, but we still use talking therapy for anxiety states, it's called cognitive behaviour therapy or CBT, and yes it has been tested by more than one randomised controlled trial (RCT). I'll set you up to see my colleague, Benjamin Shapiro, you'll find you have a lot in common, and he was first author of one of those RCTs. I'm sure he'll help you find what's behind the dark door and get rid of the incubus on your back."

***

The following week he met up with Dr Shapiro and immediately took a liking to the man. They had friends in common and shared opinions on the works of Sigmund Freud and the problems in the Middle East. It took a few minutes to deduce that his therapy had started from the moment he had sat down in a comfortable armchair set obliquely from Dr Shapiro's chair in the other corner by the window. The window was covered by a curtain made of a soft fabric coloured with a pattern of terracotta and green. The walls were all painted in a soft blue grey and the lights had been dimmed. The coffee table separating them was carrying several pots of succulent plants. The environment had obviously been designed to be relaxing and calm and was already working. After about five minutes of pleasantry the sympathetic doctor moved on to the topics of importance. "Jonathan, I would like to work with you using our first names, so please call me Benjamin. I understand you are having panic attacks and recurring nightmares. I've no doubt that the root cause is veiled but to start with can you tell me what your panic attacks feel like and what if anything triggers them. We will come to your dreams later."

"Thank you for seeing me so promptly, Benjamin, and making me feel so calm from the start.

First, you need to understand that I'm already familiar with panic attacks from a tough period of my life in the mid-1980s. My first attack was sitting in a train about to take me to deliver a lecture in Glasgow. I was suffering insomnia in those days and had only two hours sleep the night before. Suddenly I sensed that I was about to die. To the astonishment of my companions, I jumped off the train just as it was to leave the station, ran to the taxi rank and panting and sweating charged into my house terrifying my poor

14

wife. It didn't take long for my doctors to make a diagnosis, and I was heavily dosed with amitriptyline. I was confined to my bed for nearly two weeks with a filthy taste in my mouth. I then suddenly burst out crying and was inconsolable. My wife and my brothers tried to put me out of my misery by telling me how lucky I was and how marvellous my academic achievements were. This only made it worse as I knew in my heart of hearts that I was a worthless imposter. I even described myself as no better than a lump of shit in the bathroom. I was by then a serious case of anxiety-depressive illness and at risk of suicide. Anyway, to cut a long story short, after six months of therapy and the loving care of my wife, aided and abetted by a kind bank manager, I was cured. I had learnt the hard way that the earth wouldn't stop rotating on its axis if I worked less than eleven hours a day, and kept the Sabbath, at least in spirit, every weekend.

"I told you all that just to let you know that I know what a panic attack is, but what I'm experiencing now is different. They all start the same way, with a feeling of impending death, but I can control them by running round the block or by holding a lit matchstick under the palm of my hand. I'm not the least bit depressed and consider myself a lucky man. As far as triggers are concerned, they seem to be random and meaningless. For example, this morning opening the draw to find a clean pair of socks kickstarted one. Yesterday opening a new book delivered by Amazon seemed to provoke one and last Tuesday evening just putting out the rubbish bins had me running round the block. I've little doubt that a Freudian psychoanalyst might weave those random events into some sort of pattern, but I personally feel that my recurring dream might be more informative."

"Thank you, Jonathan. That was all very helpful, and you are probably right about the dream, but for the rest of this session tell me all about your life history. I promise not to use this test as a fishing rod for Freudian lapses, I simply want to learn more about you as a person, and forgiving the cliché, manage your care holistically."

For the next twenty minutes Jonathan enjoyed talking about himself uninterrupted for the first time in his life.

***

A week later for his next session with Benjamin Shapiro, after a short preamble discussing the war in Gaza, and the Saracens match with the Harlequins at the weekend, Jonathan embarked on retelling his dream that had him wake up screaming twice since their first meeting.

Benjamin listened carefully and made notes. When Jonathan had finished there was a few moments of silence whilst his psychotherapist looked in deep thought whilst sucking his pencil, after which he looked and smiled.

"Jonathan, remembering that I'm not a Freudian who claims he can interpret dreams from some accepted symbolism, you have to accept that the bulk of your dream is self-evident as I'm sure your wife has suggested. So, putting that aside we can at least agree with Freud's axiom 'Every dream has at least one point where it eludes explanation – a sort of umbilicus linking it to the unknown.' So, I think we can agree what your umbilicus into the unknown is."

Jonathan then interrupted Dr Shapiro, "Funny you should say that. I came across it last week when rereading his *Interpretation of Dreams* in priming myself for these sessions. It is of course what his hidden behind the dark door at the end of the long corridor. It reminds me of a popular song when I was a teenager, I can still remember the words of the chorus, it went like this.

'Midnight one more night without sleeping
Watching 'til that morning comes creeping
Green Door what's that secret your keeping?'
Excuse my voice but I couldn't help myself!"

Benjamin fell about laughing and responded. "At least you've got a good baritone voice for a man of your age.

16

Although I'm much younger than you, I do remember that song and I even remember the significance of the green door. Apparently during Prohibition, many restaurants painted their doors green to indicate the presence of a speakeasy. So, we now need to learn what's hiding behind your mysterious door. For a start keep a diary next to your bed and write notes on details you may have forgotten in your dreams. If that doesn't give us any more clues, I could try hypnosis. In the meantime, I'll take a blood specimen in case you've got diabetes or hepatic problems. Rarely systemic illnesses announce themselves with hallucinations, and your dreams are so detailed they even might be a form of hallucination."

# Chapter 4

## Hypnosis Breaks Down the Door

A week later Jonathan returns to Dr Shapiro's clinic feeling very anxious about his blood tests and the suggestion of a session with hypnosis. Strangely enough during that week, he had only one panic attack, triggered by taking out the rubbish bins, and there was nothing new recorded about his dream in the notebook on his bedside table. He was warmly received by his psychiatrist, who quickly reassured him about his blood tests. He then set about explaining his method of hypnosis.

"First of all, Jonathan, forget everything about theatrical hypnosis. You remain in control and there is no chance that I can persuade you to self-harm. I start with an induction procedure that does not involve swinging a pendulum in front of your eyes, it is simply my way for focussing your attention and relaxing by speaking slowly and softly. In other words, I'm trying to get you in the frame of warmth and comfort as if you were in bed just before to drop off to sleep. The process has already started by sitting you in a comfortable armchair, with dimmed lights and walls painted in muted colours. May I proceed?"

"Of course you can, I already feel relaxed," replied Jonathan.

"Right, the first thing I want of you may sound like a cliché. Imagine that you are lounging in the most relaxing setting you enjoy. Many of my clients say it would be a deckchair, on a beach, looking at a calm seascape."

"That would be a bad choice for me, I hate beach holidays, and I always suffer sunburn even if I'm sitting under a parasol. By chance this room reminds me of my favourite place for relaxing, where we go for our summer holidays. We always choose one of the Italian lakes and I always slip away from Shoshana to pay a visit to Florence and the Uffizi Gallery. In the gallery is a room about the size of your consulting room. It has the same soft light blue painted walls and only two pictures facing each other on the long walls of the rectangle. They are both the same size and both by Botticelli. They are 'The Birth of Venus' and 'Primavera', each bearing the central figure of Simonetta Vespucci, Botticelli's favourite model. The only piece of furniture in the room is the guide's chair that is always empty, and there I sit and enter a state of languor. I already feel that sense and I think your method is already taking root."

Over the next ten minutes Jonathan found himself totally relaxed and close to sleep as Dr Shapiro talked slow and softly, describing their previous encounters and outlining the content of the recurrent dream. He then suggested that Jonathan took a break and have a rest and sleep if he chooses. After a period of what seemed to be an hour or two, but was in fact five minutes, Jonathan woke up with a smile on his face.

"Welcome back" said Benjamin with a twinkle in his eye. "Have you anything to tell me?"

"Yes!" exclaimed Jonathan. "I've learnt what lays behind the door. I dreamt the dream as always but this time I learnt what was behind the door. First of all, there was a chest of drawers filled with old clothes against one wall and facing it on another wall was an elaborate *aron kodesh*, holding a *Sefer Torah*. The Torah scroll was not like the one we use in United Synagogues, but the oriental style used in Sephardi synagogues that open like a clam shell with scrolls wound round spindles secured to the case. In my dream I felt compelled to open the shell, but it wouldn't budge."

At this Dr Shapiro couldn't avoid laughing out loud, "Well done, old man, so now we have a closed box with a closed room." Having composed himself he continued,

"Seriously the symbolism is self-evident. The chest of drawers holding all your old clothes represents your past life whilst the *Sefer Torah* represents your future life. Do you really want to open the scroll? None of us can see the future and most of us know how it ends in any case. Yet, something locked in that box is a source of your panic attacks that makes you different to most other people. We could leave it there, but I have an idea that you might benefit by a visit to Kabbalist."

"A Kabbalist?" retorted Jonathan. "Are you mad? I know little about this school of Jewish mysticism, but I don't think wearing a talisman or amulet around my neck is going to frighten off my incubus."

"Trust me on this one, Jonathan. 'There are more things in heaven and earth, Horatio, than are dreamt of in your philosophy.' Rabbi Dr Nathan Adler is a qualified doctor, a fellow of the Royal College of Psychiatry, and a Charedi Jew. He lives in Stamford Hill and takes care of the sanity of the ultra-orthodox Jewish community. He has published scholarly papers on the benefits of Kabbalah. He would be the best man to open your box within your box. The scientific principle here is that because Jews have suffered from so many enemies over two millennia, from crucifixion by the Romans, beheadings by the crusaders, pogroms by the Russians, and torture by the Nazis, that their psychiatric ailments are more deeply rooted than any other race."

***

# Chapter 5

## A Trip Down Stamford Hill

Getting to Stamford Hill in Northeast London from his home in northwest London was a difficult journey for Jonathan on the next Monday morning. There was no service by the London underground and the map of bus route maps were uninterpretable. So, he set off in his car for his 10 o'clock appointment with Rabbi Adler an hour early. His journey took him along the North Circular road chocking with rush hour traffic to Stoke Newington High Street going due south to Stamford Hill. He had never been to this unprepossessing suburb before. The streets lined with post-war houses build either in the style of small Tudor manor houses punctuated by ugly concrete modernist architecture of a sub-Bauhaus persuasion. The main difference between this conurbation and any other London district were the residents all walking in a hurry to and fro as if the Messiah was on his way. Most of the men were dressed in the fashions popular in the Polish nineteenth century shtetls, identifying themselves as ultra-orthodox Jews. This uniform involved a big black hat, a long black gaberdine coat, black trousers, and black socks. They all belong to sects of the Chasidim, Hebrew for holy ones but as the sects diversified, they are now known as Charedim. Each subsect is headed by *The Rebbe,* who might be living in New York or Jerusalem. Some super-orthodox sects who interpret the Torah unquestioning the interpretations of the eighteenth-century founding father, Israel ben Eliezer, the Baal Shem Tov (master of the good name), wear their trousers tucked into white socks. On the Sabbath and holy days, they also wear a high circular fur hat. All sects have beards and long sideburns called *payot.* The posh wealthy

Charedim keep their beards and waistlines under control and can look quite elegant as they stroll to their synagogues like the *Flâneurs* of Paris, whereas their poor brethren, who probably live on handouts from the many charities supported by the wealthy, tend to be overweight, unkempt, with uncontrolled full face beards and tobacco dust on their lapels.

The women dress modestly, showing no skin up to the sleeves at their wrists. If married their hair is shaved and replaced by beautiful wigs often topped with colourful turban. They rush along the pavement pushing prams holding one or two little ones and followed by five to seven children. If it's a Friday and they are preparing for the Friday night dinner it is best to stand out of their way.

Eventually Jonathan found his way to a large pseudo-Tudor house next to the Bet Hamedrash Skiver Synagogue, on Holmleigh Road, the residence of Rabbi Dr Nathan Adler. He rang the bell, and the door was opened by a handsome young man looking about twenty-five. He was dressed in a clean white shirt open at the neck, carefully ironed black trousers with the fringes of his undervest known as *tzitzit* hanging out over his belt. He wore a black *kippah,* from which his long curled *payot* hung down to a neatly shaved beard, that would be considered fashionable even by non-Jewish young men. He gave Jonathan a big smile of welcome and said, "You must be Jonathan Tannenbaum, welcome to our humble home."

"Yes, that's me" replied Jonathan. "I've got an appointment with your father."

"That might be difficult, as my father is in New York this week."

"But I have an appointment with Dr Adler organised by Professor Benjamin Shapiro, and here is the letter of referral."

The young man took the envelope and scanned the letter, before looking up with an even bigger smile. "This letter is addressed to Rabbi Dr Nathan Adler; that's me!"

Once Jonathan had got over his surprise and embarrassment, he apologised but qualified his apology by suggesting his error could be interpreted as a back-handed compliment. Dr Adler graciously accepted the compliment and led him through a large mahogany double door into a chamber that looked more like a prayer room rather than a lounge. The far wall was facing east as it carried a modest sized *aron kodesh,* whose doors were covered with a velvet curtain embroidered with golden trees. On each side were stained glass windows also figuring trees in full bloom bearing Hebrew letters on each leaf. Along the bottom of each window Jonathan could read, with his limited reserve of Hebrew, the words *Etz Chaim,* the tree of life. The floor of the room though was covered with comfortable reclining chairs arranged in a circle, more like a luxury hotel lounge. Dr Adler led Jonathan to one of the chairs nearest to the stain glassed windows and sat himself down alongside. "Jonathan, if I may, let me explain my apparent youth. People say I look only twenty-five but in fact I'm thirty-two. I speak with an American accent because I was brought up in New York. My community in London asked my father, the Rebbe Moishe ben Aron, if he could provide them with a rabbi who could also look after the sick, in other words someone like the great philosopher, Maimonides. I was considered smart from a young age and could read sacred books both in English and Hebrew at the age of seven. At school I was always one year ahead of my grades and finished top in my exams at senior high school at the age of seventeen and was accepted as a medical student at Harvard. I graduated MD at the age of twenty-three and after my internship was completed joined a yeshiva and then a Rabbinical school. Then after receiving 'smicha', or ordination, at the age of twenty-eight, I was appointed to this post in London. You may think me a conceited braggart, but I truly believe I was gifted by Hashem to undertake this predestined role. Now let me read your referral letter before we go any further."

After reading the letter with a frown of intense concentration, he looked up again, once more with a charming smile. "Rav Tannenbaum, your visit is *Beshert,* or in English, inevitable or preordained, in that appears to bear the fingerprints of divine providence. First of all, take your name and amplify your essence during the year of your second bar mitzvah. As you know, Tannenbaum means fir tree in German, but that is not your real name, as like all other Baums it was forced upon you sometime in the past when a German speaking power had invaded Poland, and your family were living in shtetls in the forest. This would have been between 1795 and 1918 either in the grip of Prussia or Austria. Your forefathers not only lived in in a forest but were more than likely maintained the health of the trees in land granted to a nobleman by the occupying power. The fundamental principle of Kabbalah is the search for '*Ein Sof* ' the infinite emanations of unknowable God. The foundation of this search for the divine is illustrated by a tree with ten fundamental elements described as *sephirot.* These are listed from the top downward as: The Crown, the initial spark of creation, Wisdom, Understanding, Mercy, Justice, Beauty, Eternity, Glory, Foundation, and Kingdom. They can all be joined up with each other in this diagram with twenty-two paths represented by the letters of the Hebrew alphabet." Dr Adler noted that Jonathan was agitated and was about to interrupt his flow, so he held up his hand to signal that he wasn't finished yet. "Jonathan, hang on a minute, you do not need to understand any of this and in any case it's outdated. Let me return to real fir trees not of metaphysical constructs. The two-dimensional metaphysical tree was first described in the book of the 'Zohar' attributed to Moses de Leon some time in medieval

Spain of the thirteenth century. This model has been overtaken in recent years by a better mathematical three-dimensional tree. Do you know anything about fractal geometry, Jonathan?"

"As a matter of fact, I do. I published a paper a few years back about the philosophical importance of fractal geometry wherein organised systems mimic each other at different orders of magnitude."

"Correct. A tree is a perfect example of fractal geometry. The trunk with the major branches, looks mimicked in miniature by the smallest branching twigs. Furthermore, the veins on the leaves under a microscope continue the identical branching pattern. Do you know what the 'golden ratio' is?"

"Yes, it's the ratio of the length of the trunk to the length of the first branch. If I remember I think it is 1.6."

"Close. I prefer to measure it as 1.618. This not only applies to trees but is seen in the human body. The bronchial tree and all the branches of the smallest blood vessels show perfect fractal geometry in health but lose it when a cancer overgrows a healthy organ. Now consider this. In a three-dimensional tree we are imagining a number 1.618 to the power of three the first set of branches come to 4.2 on average. If you then multiply that by the ten *sephirot* you get the number forty-two. Do you recognise that number."

Sweating and pale and sensing the trigger of a panic attack, Jonathan replied, "Yes I do. We discussed this at the Friday night dinner on the eve of my second bar mitzvah. In the novel by Douglas Adams' *The Hitchhiker's Guide to the Galaxy*, he concludes that the meaning of life, the universe, and everything is forty-two. So, what's the relevance of that?"

"Douglas Adams was smarter than you think. One of the most powerful of all kabbalistic prayers is called the *Ana Beko'ach* or forty-two-letter name of God. The code to understand this prayer is a vehicle we can use to tap into the energy of creation before humanity caused the challenges of this world."

By now, Jonathan patience had been stretched to nearly breaking point.

"Dr Adler, forgive me, but all this metaphysics, however entertaining, is beginning to sound like hocus pocus or spiritual healing that's on offer at my local Baptist church."

At this point Nathan burst out laughing and went on to say, "I wondered when you'd crack! Just stay with me and I will explain what this all has in common with psychoanalysis and modern physics. One last thing that might make you think again about Kabbalah is the concept of *klippot.* They are the opposite of *sephirot.* Imagine the latter as letting the sunshine through a clean window, then *klippot* are the opposite, like cloudy soot stains. We sometimes call them 'shells' and from your notes I see that in your dream you couldn't open the doors of the *aron kodesh* as it was tightly closed like a clam shell."

That made Jonathan sit up and take notice again.

Nathan Adler continued, "Coming to the relationship with psychotherapy, we belong to the school of Carl Jung. He believed in the collective unconsciousness and described archetypes, one of which was a wise old man. That fits you perfectly and your problem might link to collective unconsciousness, another way of reading other's minds or sharing their memories. Finally let us consider the link to modern physics. We can actually see what is going on in someone's brain during panic attacks and during therapy by using an MRI scanner. We've already agreed that the networks of neurones in the brain exhibit fractal geometry. We now know that that neurones interact with each other by quantum entanglement at a subatomic level. To all but a few of the world's geniuses, that sounds like the mysticism of Schrodinger's cat thought experiment, where the cat in the box can be dead or alive at the same time. And so, we complete the circle."

Jonathan digested all that knowledge and asked the question that had been nagging him all this while. "My dear Dr Adler, that is truly interesting, but pragmatically, how does that impact on my therapy and when can we start?"

"Oh, but your treatment started the moment you entered this room. You see that *aron kodesh* between the two glass windows, it is covered with a velvet curtain. Go up and draw the curtain and open the doors of the cabinet."

Jonathan did as he was told and was amazed to see that inside the repository was a *Sefer Torah* just like in his dream.

"Now try to open the shell of the scrolls."

Unlike his dreams the halves on each side glided open as if on oiled bearings, but what he saw inside was not a Torah scroll but a sparkling clean window looking out at a strange land.

Jonathan then turned round to Dr Adler for an explanation, but the Kabbalist rabbi was no longer to be seen.

# Chapter 6

## Genesis

Jonathan walked through the window like a hand dipping in a goldfish bowl and entered a land that was cold and dark. Very quickly the sun began to rise on the east, the direction he was looking. He then saw a barren land looking red then terracotta as the sun crossed a mountain range on the horizon. He then found himself standing on the edge of a crater in the centre of a featureless desert. Suddenly he recognised where he stood. This was the Mitzpe Ramon crater in the centre of the Negev south of Beersheba in Israel. A few years ago, he stayed at a glamourous hotel perched closely to the edge of the crater where he and Shoshana enjoyed a three-day holiday in chalet with its own pool where the ibis came to drink each morning. He had learnt that the crater was not created by a meteor but was created as the putative planet Earth took shape. The hotel was called *Bereshit*. He turned round with the intention of walking back to the hotel, but there was nothing to see but a barren desert to the horizon in the west.

By this time, he warmed up as the sun reached its zenith, but in short time he was chilled as the sun settled in the west with a spectacular display across a cloudless sky. First the cobalt blue sky was stripped with the red and orange wave lengths of the spectrum as the sun dipped below the horizon, Jonathan was offered a dazzling display of indigo and violet that filled the whole of his visual field until the darkness from the east wiped out the radiance.

At that point the stars came out with their display, in the absence of light pollution, bright enough to illuminate his view of the crater. He had never seen the "milky way" as a complete arc over his head and comets and shooting stars were abundant. Within no time the sun started rising in the east and the new day shorter was shorter than the last. As so it went as each rise a setting of the sun were completed in minutes and then in seconds until Jonathan was giddy like watching fast forward on a TV screen. The sky then became a blurry blue grey when suddenly the spinning of the sun round the earth or more likely the earth around the sun, stopped and normal service was resumed at early sunrise.

Recovering from his vertigo, Jonathan looked around as was alarmed to see a man walking towards him from the south. He wore a short hessian tunic, sandals on his feet, a turban round his head, a long wooden rod in his right hand and a sack carried in his left hand thrown over his shoulder. There was no doubt he was making his way him with intent.

# Chapter 7

Yigal ben Joseph from the Tribe of Issachar
2511 years since the creation, the 17th year of the
reign Akhenaten

To his surprise the stranger threw himself at the feet of Jonathan, prostrate on the ground and delivered a greeting that sounded more like a prayer. Whatever language he was using was understood by Jonathan – that in itself seemed like a miracle. It started as follows:

"Behold, I send an angel before thee, to keep thee by the way, and to bring thee into the place which I have prepared. The Lord bless me and keep me: the Lord shine his face upon me and be gracious unto me."

Jonathan was dumbfounded and wasn't quite sure what to say, but at the same time he needed to know who this man was and if he could help him find his way home.

"Please, sir, please stand up, I'm not worthy of your blessing and I'm certainly not an angel. Please tell me who you are and perhaps we can help each other."

The stranger jumped to his feet and looked into Jonathan's eyes with a friendly smile.

He had the spark of intelligence on his face and skin the colour of horse chestnut. He was only about five foot tall, but he was muscular and fit. He then embarked on a narrative that seemed to be never ending.

"My name is Yigal ben Joseph and I work as a physician in the service of the Pharoah. I am from the tribe of Issachar, one of the twelve clans of Israelites. We call ourselves Israelites as we are descendants of the sons of Jacob who changed his name to Israel. We can trace our ancestry back 1,250 years because it is written on the walls of our palaces, our tombs and the papyruses held in the great library in Amarna on the east coast of the great river Nile. The history of the Israelites is intertwined with the history of the Pharaohs. Joseph was known as Imhotep in the language of the ancients. He was the vizier, architect, astrologer, and chief minister to Djoser, who reigned as the second king of Egypt's third dynasty. He was the architect of the step pyramid built at the necropolis of Saqqara. Imhotep's high standing in Djoser's court is confirmed by an inscription bearing his name on a statue of Djoser at the site of the Saqqara pyramid that can be seen to this day. Imhotep was responsible for saving Egypt from a seven-year famine, having built the massive underground silos that can be found adjacent to the Djoser pyramid complex at Saqqara, thus saving Egypt from a seven-year famine. He bought up all the land for Pharaoh by selling the grain he stored during the seven years that preceded the famine and that explains how the Pharaohs became so powerful. As a reward Pharaoh gave Imhotep his signet ring, dressed him in fine linen and put a gold chain around his neck. He was given a chariot to ride around Egypt as second in command and he was given a wife Asenath, daughter of the priest Potiphar. From thereon, the story follows exactly the well charted history of Imhotep that is carved in stone and inscribed in papyri. At some point the princely decedents of Imhotep contributed to list of future Pharaohs, Amenhotep I to III who were followed by Tuthmose IV the grandfather of our mighty and beloved King Amenhotep IV, who changed his name Akhenaten who married our queen, of fabulous beauty, Neferneferuaten. Akhenaten changed his wife's name to Nefertiti, that meant *behold a beautiful lady comes before us.* Whereas our pharaoh's new name meant, *dedicated to the Aton, the sun disc.* The changing of their names was the trigger for the cataclysm that was to fall upon us. Thirteen years into his reign, whilst walking alone in his private garden in his palace at Memphis, he heard a loud voice coming from the sky, he turned to see it's source and found himself blinded by the sun disc. He dropped to his knees and bent his head. His sight came back but the voice became louder. Later he recorded the words writing in his own hands on a sheet of the best vellum, these words.

I am the Lord Your God, no one must know my true name so you and your followers will call me The Name. I am the one and only God and I will replace all the fraudulent gods that have been invented over the years since my last true servant, Joseph, came to the land of the Nile, I know as Mizrahim. You will leave Memphis and build a temple for my worship in land east of the Nile where I will show you. You will start each day with prayers looking to the east as my orb rises from behind the Mountains of the Moon.

And so it came to pass, a new city, with a new temple dedicated to The Name, was built at Amarna a long way south of Memphis at the feet of the Mountains of the Moon. The temple and all its engravings showed images of our king and queen worshipping the sun disc and its rays. The simple souls amongst us assumed that the sun disc was God himself, whereas Akhenaten believed that the blinding disc was simply the doorway to another kingdom that governed all the nations of the world and blessed those countries who accepted his Kingdom of Kingdoms with bounties of grain, gold, and freedom from plagues. In the seventeenth year of his reign as he started to feel the weight of responsibilities, he made Nefertiti Queen Consort all but a Pharoah herself. Their oldest son, Amenhotep, was named as the heir to the throne and his second born, Tuthmose, was honoured with the title High Priest of the Aten. Tuthmose, took his duties seriously. He understood the enormity of worshipping one god governing all the peoples of the world and set about codifying a list for good behaviour that would please the Aten and wrote hymns to glorify *The Name*. He also orchestrated ceremonies for the seasons of the year that would please *The Name* to cause the Nile to flood and water the land that grew the grain that fed the people. As well as the fertility of the land, their God was interested in the fertility of their womenfolk. A young wife who wanted to please her husband with a first born would sacrifice two doves to please *The Name.*

"Before the breeding season of their goats and their herds of cattle, the men would bring one of a herd to sacrifice at the next festival at the temple. In the seventeenth year of his reign, Akhenaten died and his regent, Nefertiti, took over his role. This was not taken kindly by the other Royal Clans in the land supporting the children of the Pharaoh's other wives and courtesans. Within two years Nefertiti and Amenhotep died of the plague, but I, one of his humble doctors, suspected they were poisoned. This was the end of the Amarna lineage and at a gathering of all the nobility of the land it was agreed that Tutankhamun, the son of one of Akhenaten's courtesans, would be crowned as their king. Again, in my suspicious mind, I thought the choice was because he was a lad of sixteen or seventeen years, who could easily be manipulated by the council of twelve high ranking attendants of the court of the royal family. Their first action was to move the capital back to Memphis and restore a polytheistic religious centre at Thebes.

Friends in high places alerted us that Tutankhamun had raised an army of a thousand foot soldiers led by a hundred bowmen in chariots. They were making the way to Amarna to destroy our temple and drive the believers of the new faith of the sun disc out of the land. Having no doubt that this would lead to murder, rape, and pillage, Thutmose our high priest spoke with *The Name,* who demanded that we take our valuables and food enough for a week and make our way to the Saqqara necropolis on the west side of the Nile where they could rest for a while, but to leave spies behind, one from each clan, to see what this army might do once they'd razed Amarna to the ground. Would they leave it at that or follow them to take us back as slaves? The spies must be fleet of foot and sharp with their eyes. That clearly meant me to represent the tribe of Issachar, as I always won the annual races of the sun at the equinox on the first of Av. As the tribes traipsed away, those left behind took off their travelling garments and covered their nakedness with sackcloth and applied shackles round our ankles without chains. This way we were disguised as slaves. Once we heard the sound of marching men and the neighing of horses, we turned round and greeted the vanguard of the legion as if they were our saviours. To our surprise, instead of searching the empty streets of Amarna or preparing to chase after the fugitives, they pitched tents, lit campfires, hobbled the chariot horses, and rested. Along with the other spies, I was dragged to fall at the feet of the commanding officer in the headquarter marquee. He was a giant of a man, aged about forty, wearing elaborate armour and the colours of the north and the regiment of Ra, the pharaoh's praetorian guard. Instead of impressing me in all his glory, I found myself looking at a sick man. His complexion was grey, and he was sweating. I discreetly looked him over and observed red nodules just below the skirt of leather straps. He had all the stigmata of the plague. Glancing around his attendants I noticed two other senior officers barely able to stand and holding themselves up with their speers. We were then cross-examined by an interpreter who assumed we were Hebrew slaves who couldn't speak Egyptian. We all gave the same story that we were left behind to starve whilst our masters and their families escaped by running away to the east, climbing the Mountains of the Moon to confuse Pharaoh's army who might have assumed they would take the easy route to the west. We listened carefully as the talked amongst themselves. They obviously had a serious outbreak of the plague that had decimated their legions and had decided to rest here to recover. In the meantime, they would send scouts to explore the tracks left by our exodus. Others would search the buildings of Amarna and search for objects of value that would please Pharoah and the court, and some of the booty would be distributed amongst the foot soldiers to maintain their morale. After that they should set fire to all that was flammable rather than wasting time razing the buildings to the ground. That night we sat in a circle, fed flat bread and guarded by two pikemen whilst we slept.

When our two guards were distracted by the arrival of their food and changed places with two other foot soldiers, we quietly agreed that one of us would run after our brethren to pass on the intelligence we had gathered. I was chosen and slipped away, running at a steady pace westward towards the step pyramid at Saqqara. I hadn't got far before an arrow from one of the Egyptian soldiers, who was controlling the westernmost boundary of their camp, transfixed my body."

***

At this point Yigal ben Joseph became pixelated and faded away. Once more Jonathan is alone in the desert. A few days pass rapidly once again repeating the display, with Jonathan sensing that he is at the epicentre of a huge beach ball with segments of all the colours of the spectrum. Normality returns suddenly and Jonathan remains on the edge of the crater. He sees something out the corner of his eye that looks like a sandstorm coming from the south.

This transforms into a multitude of men and women, led by a tall man wearing a long white robe and bearing a long black beard and a golden staff in his right hand. He raises his rod and the horde come to a halt to allow their leader to introduce himself to the humble Professor Tannenbaum.

# Chapter 8

## The High Priest of Aten

The leader of the flock examined Jonathan from *haute et basse* and decided to honour this humble man with another long monologue.

"My name is Tuthmose, and I am the high priest of the Aten. After their deaths, the boy Tutankhamen, the only son of Akhenaten, whose mother was the whore whose name will not be spoken, became king. He had no wisdom of his own and regents from the sects of Amun-Ra, Osiris, Horus, Thoth, and Hathor, denounced the followers of the one and only god, the Aten. They sent their men at arms to deface our temple and destroy the images of Aten. I, at the age of sixteen, had my hair shorn and was anointed a priest to serve the forbidden god. My father, Tuthmose, at that time, following the death of Akhenaten, had been anointed high priest by my mother. He decreed that effigies of gods were not to be worshipped but the one true god cannot be looked at in the face lest you become blinded. Following the destruction of our temple, we who were living in Amarna were subject to heavy taxes and forbidden to worship the orb on pain of death. Many of our young men were drafted into the armies of the new king and many of our daughters were taken into slavery. We could not protect them as we were not allowed to bear arms on pain of death. Then swarms of locusts from the dark lands of Nubia destroyed all our crops and famine led to the deaths of many of our little ones. Plague struck us again and I lost my father and my young brother Amenhotep, who were buried in humble coffins alongside the shrine of my noble mother as all our gold and precious woods and stones had been taken as taxes by the army of the boy king. Finally, the regents of the

"

upper and lower land of Egypt decreed that all those who worshipped the Aten must renounce their faith and return to the worship of the old gods lest they die. Their messengers alerted us that the armies of Tutankhamen from Memphis in the north and Thebes in the south would arrive the next day. I spoke unto my people and offered them a choice to either obey the edict of the king and stay or join me to flee from this place to find a place of safety in the desert west of the Nile. Forty families agreed to follow me.

I then ordered all the women to make flat bread to take on our journey, enough food for eight days. We had nine camels to carry water. The night before the arrival of the detachments of the king's army arrived, our small procession of forty men, their families and a hundred of our loyal servants, crossed the river to the west and turned north to follow the river in the direction of Saqqara. Some of our servants who had come from Nubia were sent east up into the mountainous zone that had formed a protective bowel for our beloved royal city of Amarna, carrying flares and beacons to provide a decoy when the soldiers of the king arrived. They were well rewarded and hoped to escape to the south in a hazardous journey back to the land of their birth.

"We reached the necropolis at Saqqara after walking for nearly eight days. Although the women and children took turns on riding the camels, the beasts themselves were exhausted and our supplies of bread, water, and wine depleted. The local villages knew nothing of our plight and assumed we were either nomads or traders who often past along this route. They were happy to supply us with enough food and water to continue our journey to the flat lands, east of the Nile delta. We had no idea how long it would take for the king's soldiers to catch up with us. My plan was to find a way across the Reed Sea of the delta and turn northward to the land of the Canaanites and the tribes who lived east of the Jordan River. Although part of the Egyptian empire, they had many grievances, and I planned to convert them to our ways and raise an army to conquer the lower kingdom. But first we had to find a way of crossing to the other side of the great river, nay the Reed Sea, that has sustained the lives of generation after generation to the beginning of time thank to the will and blessing of our Lord, the Aten. The Nile delta is known as the Reed Sea because most of the rivulets run through freshwater marshland rich with the papyrus reed, but the most western branch of the delta is known as the Canopic mouth, and that is our first challenge. Once we cross there, our guides, Caleb, son of Jephunneh and Joshua, son of Nun, know of a secret route through the marshes where the water never rises above knee level.

There is no bridge across the Canopic and the boatmen who normally carry traders across had all taken their craft out to sea for fear of Pharoah's army alerted by messengers on fast horseback. All that was left to me was to kneel down and pray. The moment my knees touched the ground my prayers were foreseen, first a flash of brilliant light due north of where we were gathered followed by a thunderclap, so loud it shook the land we stood on. This was followed by a mushroom shaped black cloud that grew and grew until the sun was blotted out and night fell. Then the miracle ensued as the waters of the mouth of the Canopic river were sucked out to sea and a patch of dry ground the width of one hundred men appeared in the Reed Sea, and I was able to lead my people across the marshes on the other side. Once all my tribes were on safe land, I turned round to witness another miracle.

The vanguard of Pharoah's contingent arrived at the spot we had just abandoned and paused in a state of bewilderment. Not far behind them were the chariots of their officers who kept up the chase, screaming at the laggards to follow. Once the throng were halfway across, there was a sudden thunderous noise of gushing water as the sea sent its tsunami back to the land that it had previously covered. The Israelites looked on in horror, taking no pleasure in seeing their enemies drowning in front of their eyes.

"Joshua ben Nun, our guide, estimated that walking at the pace of the slowest it would take eight days to reach Pithom in the land of Goshen, the land that was gifted to our patriarch, Joseph, after he saved the land by storing seven years' worth of grain in the silos around the step pyramid. Fortunately, as if pre-empted by Hashem, there were eight pastures of dry land each a day's walk away, for pitching our tents and resting through the nights. These zones were free of serpents that favour the wetlands adjacent to each branch of the delta.

"And so it came to pass that after eight days we could rest in the narrow stretch of fertile land near the coastline at Sin and the desert of Sinai. We then turned south and marched around the Great Bitter Lake to enter the wilderness of Shur. After discussions with my guide Joshua ben Nun, we decided it would be safer walking in a south-east direction along the coast of the Red Sea, rather than walking due east through the desert where we could run out of water and easily get lost. We could then turn north-east at the tip of the Sinai peninsula, a distance of ten days walking at a pace of thirty furlongs a day. We set off on this section of their voyage with adequate supplies of food and water carried on the backs of a procession of camels early one morning late in the month of Nisan. All went well for five days until suddenly we were hit by a khamsin wind blowing up from the south-west. This burning sandstorm forced up to pitch our tents. The heat drove some of my followers mad, as well as draining our supplies of water. Fights broke out over trivial matters, such as theft of food, and some ended with mortal wounds. Yet we had to keep moving once the khamsin had blown itself out. By the time we reached the tip of the Sinai peninsula, the multitudes were rioting, my leadership was challenged, and food and water were running out. My people broke into factions, some wanting to go back to Egypt, and others blaming Hashem and started praying to the idols of the heretics. When all seemed lost a sudden thunderstorm broke out with lightning striking the peak of the mountain that overlooked the coupling of the waters from the Red Sea with the waters from the gulf of Aqaba. Once again, I heard the voice of Hashem, this time ordering me to climb up the fearful rock face that led to the peak of the mountain that acting like a lightening attractor. I equipped myself with two soft clay tablets and a stylus and had a quiet word with Aaron my older brother. He was the leader of my tribe, the Levites, that happen to include a subsect of Sicarii. The Sicarii were useful in controlling riots with the help of the daggers they hid in their robes. I reached the peak of the mountain in the heart of a storm with thunder and lightning, then suddenly all became quiet and peaceful. Then again, I had heard the words of Hashem telling me where our final destination was to be and how we should behave to deserve this paradise.

"Rod in hand I strode off through the foothills and rock falls of the mountain of the Sinai until I found a nice dry cave, equipped with food and water for one lunar month, where I could be inspired by Hashem to write a code of behaviour that would bring peace and comfort for the tribes and be worthy of the land we had been promised. The last thing I did at the will of Hashem, was to change my name from the Egyptian tongue from Tuthmose to the Hebrew equivalent, Moses.

"Here you can see the first draft of what I thought might be called the Ten Decrees. I thought ten would be a good number as they could count them off on their fingers." At that point the man Moses paused and passed Jonathan two inscribed wax tablets inscribed with a list of directives that would bring peace and prosperity to the tribes of the Israelites.

1. There is only one God and that's Hashem.

2. You must not make idols and pray to them.

3. You must not try to discover the name of our God.

4. You must have a day of rest every seven days for your prayers to Hashem.

5. Show respect to your mother and father.

6. You must not murder.

7. You must not lay down with someone else's wife.

8. You must not steal.

9. You must not tell lies about others of the children of Israel.

10. Don't compare your belongings with your neighbours with envy.

***

After forty days I returned to the encampments of the twelve tribes and was well received. Aaron then organised a gathering of the elders of the tribes to hear the ten commandments and learn of the locus of the "promised land". Our guide, Joshua ben Nun, would lead us to Canaan that was blessed with very fertile soil, good supplies of clean water from the mountain range at its north-east region, and some very nice sandy beaches of the Great Sea. During the time away from my flock I allowed my beard to grow so that I looked an impressive figure as I once again appeared upon the rocky platform that overlooked the camping sites of the twelve tribes facing every adult man and woman filling the desert land as far as I could see. Aaron appeared by my side together with a herald who blew three loud musical notes on a ram's horn. *Tekiya, tekiya, tekiya-a-a-a!*

As I am shy of speaking in public, Aaron who had a booming voice, cried out the messages from Hashem delivered by his agent, Moses, the father of the Israelites.

On occasions like this, relays of heralds ran from the front lines carrying the messages.

As the words of the Ten Decrees reached the periphery of assembly, some grumbling could be heard. Numbers nine and ten were being challenged. When this got back to me, I answered that this was only the first draft, and the final version would be worked out by a presidium of the patriarchs of the twelve tribes. Once that was settled, second on the agenda were the plans for taking the land of the Canaanites. It was agreed that each tribe would send their master spy with the task to seek out the lay of the land. The tribe of Issachar had tragically lost their leading master spy early in their journey from the step pyramid and had to offer a recent recruit. These were the orders they carried as they left the camps and made their way north-east to the land of the Philistines.

1. Go through the Negev and then the mountain region and see what the land is like and whether the people living there are strong or weak, few or many.

2. Do their cities have walls around them or not?

3. Is the soil rich or poor? Does the land have trees or not.

4. Bring back some fruit of the land as this is the season when grapes were beginning to ripen.

A second command was sent out to all the goldsmiths and craftsmen to design and create an ark worthy of carrying the tablets of the covenant of Hashem once they start marching to the promised land.

So, the men explored the land from the Desert of Zin to the border of Hamath. They went through the Negev and came to Hebron. When they came to the Eshkol Valley, they cut off a branch with only one bunch of grapes on it. They carried it on a pole between two of them. They also brought some pomegranates and figs. Forty days later, they came back to Moses, Aaron, and the whole community of Israelites at their camping ground at Kadesh in the Desert of Paran. This is what they reported to Moses: "We went to the land where you sent us. It really is a land flowing with milk and honey. Here's some of its fruits, for example. But the people who live there are strong, and the cities have walls and are very large. But there is also an unexpected threat from hostile tribes along the way. The Amalekites live in the Negev, the Hittites, Jebusites, and Amorites live in the mountain region. And finally, the Canaanites who live along the coast of the Great Sea and all along the Jordan River. Caleb, son of Jephunneh, from the tribe of Judah spoke first, "Let's go now and take possession of the land. We should be more than able to conquer it." Joshua ben Nun, from the tribe of Ephraim, agreed and then told the people to be quiet and listen to Moses. But before Moses spoke the other ten spies joined in. "We can't attack those people! They're too strong for us!"

"The land we explored is one that devours those who live there. All the people we saw there are very tall."

"We felt as small as grasshoppers, and that's how we must have looked to them."

Moses banged his rod on the ground to silence them and then asked Aaron to advise on the best response. "First of all, before we jump to any decisions, we need a census of able men over the age of twenty and an audit of those bearing weapons to judge our strength."

There was a murmuring of agreement in the gathering and so it was done, tribe by tribe. They reconvened two days later and a herald from each tribe called out the numbers, whilst Aaron inscribe them on a beeswax tablet. The total came to 600,000 men able to bear arms, but there's the rub, how many held arms. The audit of weaponry was disappointing. Only one in ten carried a knife or a spear. Then there was the issue of siege engines breaking through strongholds or walled cities. Or siege-ladders to climb over the walls. It would also be impossible to starve the defenders to give up as they would have more water and food than we could carry. Moses' promise that God would provide was accepted by the bellicose men and scorned by the sceptics almost in equal numbers. In the end a compromise was agreed when Joshua ben Nun suggested a reconnoitre to plan the best route for an invasion should it be agreed. He would lead a small group of armed men to study the terrain along the southern border of Canaan whilst Caleb would take a group alongside of the river Jordan to determine if an attack from the east flank would take the Canaanites by surprise. That might take three lunar months, during which time the men could build their strength, casting their bronze swords, build siege towers, and battering rams.

***

Jonathan Tannenbaum remained under his arc of the rainbow wondering how much longer this would last. He wasn't hungry or thirsty but simply bored. Suddenly the rainbow display stopped and was replaced by the starlit sky, but not for long. Clouds drifted in from the north, blotting out the starlight until the world became pitch-black. Not sure if he was blind or not, he fumbled in an inside pocket of his jacket and pulled out his iPhone. Fumbling in the dark he eventually slid his finger diagonally across the face of the phone and turned on the built-in torch and shone it at the ground. Just as he had reassured himself that he was not blind a young man dressed in leather armour threw himself at his feet and started babbling away. "Oh, angel with the flaming sword what message does my Lord have for his servant, Joshua ben Nun. Shall we take Canaan from the south, or should our battalions take Jericho from the east? We have 600,000-foot soldiers and as many bronze swords and breastplates like I wear today."

By this time Jonathan had latched on to the fact that he had a walk on part in Biblical history, and assuming his teachers at his Hebrew Sunday School were correct he could tell the future. He decided there and then to play his part and encourage the Nun son to stick to the script of the scriptures. He gave a cough to clear his throat and then spoke out with the authority of an archangel. "Listen carefully, Joshua ben Nun, make no attempt to conquer the land of the Canaanites at this time. Your foot-soldiers are weak of arm and have learnt no skills of warfare. The bronze of your swords will break against the shields of your enemy. The walls around Jericho are too strong to be broken down. You need your womenfolk to give birth to another 600,000 boys who will be trained to become the most fearsome of warriors of all time. Over the next forty years, the Canaanites will become complacent, decadent, and corrupt. They will neglect the maintenance of the walls around their cities and become bloated by their rich sources of milk and honey. I have seen into the future. If you obey the advice of the lord, Hashem, the walls of Jericho will come tumbling down and all the land from the river to the Great Sea will become the promised land of Israel for a thousand years!"

Joshua heard those words of the Lord and took it upon himself to carry the message back to the encampment in the Negev. Caleb was recalled from his reconnoitre from his camp just south of the sea of the harp where it fed the great river Jordan. An emergency meeting of the presidium of the twelve tribes was called by Moses and Aaron and the prophesies of the angel with the fiery sword were accepted. For the next forty years the children of Israel lived as nomads, guiding their flocks to pastures in the lands of Negev and the mountainous lands east of the river Jordan. The womenfolk listened to the words of the angel; to be fruitful and multiply and to encourage this praiseworthy injunction, the menfolk were allowed to take four wives each. All this time the ark of the holy covenant led the way and the numbers of priests, cousins or nephews of Moses and Aaron, increased in numbers as to create an elite clan of Kohanim within the tribe of the Levites.

# Chapter 9

Tannenbaum at the Fall of Lachish
3059 years after creation or Gregorian year
701BCE

Suddenly Jonathan Tannenbaum found himself back sitting in a comfortable armchair back in Dr Adler's sitting room. He looked at the clock on the wall above the cabinet of curiosities and noted that he had only been away for one hour, whereas his hallucinations seemed to have lasted a lifetime. Nevertheless, he felt very calm and relaxed. He then looked round and saw Dr Adler sitting next to him with sphinx-like smile on his lips. "Well, Jonathan, how did you enjoy your voyage from the creation to the Israelite spies described in your bar mitzvah *Sedra?*" he asked.

"It was wonderful, and I seem to feel ecstatic following that experience. Forgive me though, what was the point of that immersive retelling of the Bible story?"

"Let me explain," responded the good doctor. "A fundamental teaching of the Kabala, as I've explained already in simple terms, is the links between *sephirot* and the three dimensions of your tree of life, has a fourth dimension by which a tree becomes a forest. Continuing with this analogy, trees communicate with each other by their roots that represent a mirror image of the fractal dimensions of the branches, twigs, and leaves above ground. They communicate in a way like the neurons of the brain. One acorn planted in the soil a thousand years ago can, if the climate allows it, be the founding father of this forest. Translate that into human terms, our forefathers established extended families that intermarried and built of tribes and those tribes coalesced into a distinct race. As a race we share a common history, we share our memories, and we share the praise or blame for the good and bad behaviour of our forefathers in the past. Sigmund Freud called this "Collective History". Sometime in the past, one of your ancestors was guilty of a crime that had terrible consequences for other members of our race. We will explore the past in hourly sessions to see if we can identify the point in time when this transgression occurred and see if you can redeem your distant relative by reversing the consequences of that misdemeanour. Next week you will witness the Assyrian attack on the Judah following their success in conquering the northern kingdom of Israel.

***

Jonathan started to look forward to his next "treatment" with trepidation as he primed himself for his next journey through the looking glass via the cabinet of curiosities. A quick visit to the British Museum revealed these words translated from a wall panel relief from Nineveh attributed to King Sennacherib after his conquest of Lachish in 701 BCE.

*Hezekiah, King of Judah, would not submit to my yoke, I came up against him, and by force of arms and by the might of my power I took forty-six of his strong-fenced cities; and of the smaller towns which were scattered about, I took and plundered a countless number. From these places I took and carried off 200 persons, old and young, male and female, together with horses and mules, asses and camels, oxen and sheep, a countless multitude.*

Once the formalities were complete and young Dr Adler had disappeared, he found himself on a grassy knoll facing a heavily fortified city on a hill about 200 metres away. The spectacle he was witnessing would have been difficult to process even in slow motion, but the tumult across his whole field of vision appeared to be acted in disjointed high speed.

It appeared like hundreds of men, maybe soldiers, prisoners of war or slaves, were picking up rocks from a quarry at the right limit of his visual field. They then scurried like ants leaving their nest to the left limit of his visual field, the city with the fortifications. Instead of dropping their rocks at the foot of the hill bearing the city they started building a carpet of stones about 100 metres to the right. As the heap increased in size a pattern began to emerge, they were building a siege ramp from tail to head. As soon as the defenders understood what was happening, they started shooting arrows or throwing spears at those in the front of the ascending slope. This then demonstrated the cunning of the attack. At the front of the ramp stood a line of soldiers protecting the builders with iron shields taller than the men. As they got closer and closer another line of soldiers carried their shields above the heads of the workmen. Inevitably some were hit and fell off the ramp but there was no shortage of slaves to fill their posts. Once the leading flat face of the ramp reached the walls of the fortress, all the builders and their protective shield holders scampered down under a fusillade of burning arrows.

There was a pause whilst the siege engines were lined up three abreast. First the battering rams and behind them the siege towers carrying platforms for their bowmen to counterattack the defenders. The fighting was vicious, and bodies were flying down off the battlements of the city walls, as many of those falling off the siege towers and the ramp.

In the final stage of this frontal attack, wooden beams were laid on top of the stones, where the huge battering ram, requiring twenty men to carry it, was positioned. The large heavy wooden beam with a metal tip battered the walls by being swung back and forth, like a pendulum suspended on metal chains. In no time the wall was shattered, and the assailants stormed through the gap screaming and beating their swords on their shields,

Meanwhile, Jonathan, from his lookout, noted battalions of Assyrian soldiers rising like serpents from the tall grassland at the foot of the hillside bearing the besieged city and making their way around to attack the city from the rear.

Now the defenders were fighting on two fronts, and it was easy to guess who the victors were. Bodies were being thrown over the battlements after decapitation with the carcasses followed by their heads. A signature emblem of Assyrian warfare. The bodies piled up into a slope building up against the western wall of the of the rocky mound supporting the fortress city of Lachish facing Jonathan. Everything then went quiet and there was a pause in the Cinerama playing out in the visual field of the one observer.

Within minutes the anthill was disturbed again, and hundreds of slaves were driven by whips and rods to start digging a trench about the size of a football pitch and deep enough to hide the heads of the gravediggers. When complete, and without any ceremony, all the corpses together with their heads were shovelled into the pit. And then, as if adding insult to injury, the Assyrian legionnaires threw the bodies of living pigs on top of the pile of the Israelite warriors. Once the surface of the mound of squealing pigs reached the top of the pit, the slaves with their shovels, covered the whole writhing hillock with the stone and soil from the excavation.

With their work done, the slaves were chained one to another at their ankles and marched off to the Assyrian's camps somewhere at the east side of the razed city of Lachish.

Jonathan assumed that was the end of the story, but suddenly something inexplicable transpired. The victorious soldiers started screaming and turning to face Jonathan's lookout, started charging up the foot of his hillock, as if they had spotted him as a spy. He was stupefied into inertia but then realised that the hoard weren't running at him but running away from a colony of black rats, each the size of a bulldog.

Once they were fifty metres away, Jonathan found himself slipping back through the looking glass into Dr Adler's sitting room.

***

Once he had recovered from his adventure, Dr Adler with the smile of a sphinx completed the story. "The miracle you have just witnessed was the initiation of the bubonic plague that decimated the Assyrian army, and persuaded King Sennacherib to give up his plans for taking Jerusalem and adding Judah to his conquest of Israel. Come and see me next week and learn how the Babylonians succeeded where the Assyrians failed.

# Chapter 10

## The Fall of the Temple to the Babylonians
## The 9th of Av
## 2945 years after creation or Gregorian year 587 BCE

Once again Jonathan made his way to the British Museum, this time to study the fall of King Solomon's temple, yet once again the story starts at the garrison town of Lachish.

This was the first consequence of the rebellion of Judah, a vassal nation within the Babylonian Empire, against the mighty masters. The town had reverted to Judean control, only to fall again to Nebuchadnezzar in his campaign against Judah in 588–587 BCE during the reign of Hezekiah. Lachish served an important protective function in defending Jerusalem and the interior of Judea because the easiest way to get a large attacking army up to Jerusalem was to approach from the coast. To lay siege to Jerusalem an invading army would first have to take Lachish, which guarded a mountain pass. In January 588 BCE the Babylonian army placed Jerusalem under blockade and began the destruction of outlying strong points, taking them one by one until finally only Lachish and Azekah were left standing. The fall of Azekah was movingly illustrated in one of the "Lachish letters", in which an officer in charge of an observation post writes to the garrison commander in Lachish that the fire signals of Azekah can no longer be seen.

*"And let my lord know that we are watching for the signals of Lachish, according to all the indications which my lord hath given, for we cannot see Azekah."*

The city that once occupied an area of twenty acres was finally razed to the ground shortly before the conquest of Jerusalem, leaving a huge mound of rubble he had explored in the past.

Jonathan bought a facsimile of the ceramic "letters" in the museum shop before making his way to the nearby British Library at St Pancras, a peaceful sanctuary to study the interpretations of the Biblical descriptions of the fall of the first temple in Jerusalem.

It appeared that the prophet Jeremiah had warned the Judeans of impending doom for years. Judea was living with a false sense of security. They somehow felt that they would be able to rebel against the power of Babylon and sustain the rebellion. They deluded themselves that Egypt would protect them, thinking that their southern neighbour preferred to confront Babylon north of Jerusalem rather fighting them on their own borders. However, Egypt was not willing to spill one drop of Egyptian blood on behalf of Judea. Another delusion was that somehow the Babylonians would forget about them. However, the king of Babylon was not about to let Judea slip out of his orbit. He came with his whole army to put down the rebellion – and he came with cruelty, vengeance, and determination. Nebuchadnezzar came from the north and invaded the outskirts of Judea. By the early part of the summer his army had encamped around Jerusalem. He cut off the city and systematically tightened the noose around Jerusalem. On the ninth day of the month of Tammuz the walls of the city were breached, and the Babylonian army poured through. Within a month they had destroyed all pockets of Judean resistance. Tens of thousands died in the siege, which brought on famine and pestilence, and then by sword and fire. Those who could do so fled. However, the Babylonians had anticipated that and herded escapees into giant slave camps, from where they were transported into exile in Babylon.

Having learnt all that, Jonathan was at a loss about what he might learn by another episode through the looking glass.

***

A week later when he was once more in Dr Adler's sitting room, he was alarmed to learn that his next time travel would involve his active participation rather than as a passive witness.

"My dear Professor Tannenbaum, your next visit will not only be meaningful to you but might also avoid a wormhole in time and space that could extinguish 2,500 years in the history of the children of Israel. For this you will need to carry these three items with you that will galvanize your mission."

Jonathan was nonplussed by the gifts he would be carrying into the sixth century BCE and didn't know whether to cry with fear or laugh at the farce. The items were a miner's helmet bearing a flashlight, a toy Jedi lightsaber from Star Wars and a Jericho 941, a semi-automatic pistol. Before he had time to express his incredulity, Dr Adler continued. "You must think I'm insane, but the value of the two stage props will become apparent when you cross the timeline. As for the pistol, await your instructions. On this trip you will hear instructions from the clouds in the sky. Please open the cabinet and enter the past."

Jonathan felt himself duty-bound to make his journey. Once again, his step into the past led him to a platform whose view was familiar. He was looking across a beautiful valley of Hinnom, from the west side that provided the best view of the ancient walls around the old city of Jerusalem. On many occasions he had been invited by the Hebrew University of Jerusalem as a visiting professor of philosophy to spend a week or so running classes for both undergraduates and postgraduates. He was always treated as an honorary visitor by the Jerusalem Foundation and enjoyed the privilege of staying in their guest house *Mishkenot Sha'ananim.* Every morning whilst sleeping there, the first thing he would do on awaking, was to open the shutters of his suite and admire the ancient walls across the valley glowing like gold as they reflected the rising sun. He would then have his coffee and croissants on the terrace outside enjoying the spectacular colour scheme of the emerald green of the valley, the gold of the walls and the cobalt blue of the sky. But on this occasion, there were two icons missing from the view of the walls. On his far left the *Migdal David* (Tower of David) was missing. Although it was assumed it had been there since the days of King David, it was in fact the tower from a mosque during the Ottoman era. The other obvious absent mark was the roof of the Armenian Church that should have been a little to the right of his visual field. He therefore assumed that behind his back there would be a plateau that in the future would bear his much-loved guest house. It this case he was correct but what he hadn't predicted was a company of seven Israelite soldiers wearing iron helmets, leather chest-plates bearing iron inserts, a skirt of hanging leather wattles and leather shin guards. They carried long spears in their right hands and short swords hanging from their waists. Their left arm was hidden by a long metal shield bearing the six-pointed star of David, the *Magen Dovid.* Their eyes were focused on a fight that became apparent at the base of the western wall of the old city. It didn't take Jonathan long to figure out that this was the beginning of the siege of Jerusalem by the Babylonian army of Nebuchadnezzar and that these soldiers were on duty as surveillance patrols. Suddenly a voice thundered out from the clear blue sky above. "Jonathan, your role is to rescue the Arc of the Covenant. Now you must put on your helmet, switch on the torch-light and activate the Jedi Sabre sword." The Israelite foot soldiers were terrified by the voice from above and then turned round to see a tall man with a golden halo on his head and a flaming sword in his right hand. All seven prostrated themselves flat upon the ground facing this "angel of the Lord" and chanting in unison the prayer-*Shema* prayer.

*"Hear, O Israel: Adonai is our God, Adonai in One! Blessed is God's name; His glorious kingdom is for ever and ever! And you shall love Adonai your God with all your heart, with all your soul, and with all your might."*

For a while Jonathan was at a loss on what to do next, when the captain of the small company lying on the ground, showed his courage by lifting his head and shaking with fear, asked the obvious question. "Oh, Angel of Hashem, I am your humble servant, Eliezer ben Levi, you find us at a time of despair. The Babylonian army has Jerusalem besieged and our people are starving. We are a small group who were sent out through a secret tunnel under the walls to forage for food. We can't last much longer and then the barbarians will sack the city, tear down the temple, and take any survivors to the land between the rivers as slaves. Hear our prayers and may our merciful father save us."

By this time the other Israelite soldiers raised themselves from the ground and knelt with their hands clasped as if begging for help. Jonathan had tears in his eyes as he knew the outcome that was predestined.

"I am indeed a messenger for Hashem and one of the hosts of fearsome angels. I have come to you not to battle with the Babylonian legions, but to save the Ark of the Covenant. This is more important than winning a battle, because we know in the future the Babylonian Empire will melt away like the ice on Mount Hermon, yet with the Ark of the Covenant, the children of Israel will live forever, and a second temple will be built in Jerusalem. So, your role is to follow me into the temple and take the Ark of the Covenant to another place where it can be hidden until Jerusalem is built again and a second temple will rise from the ashes. Have no fear. If you walk by my side no one will dare to stand in our way." That was enough to convince ben

Levi and his merry men once they had recovered from their shock. And led by "Archangel" Tannenbaum, the crossed the valley of Hinnom and made their way up to the foot of the walls of the city aiming for the Dung Gate the nearest entry to the Temple Mount. All along the way the Babylonian militants moved aside having difficulty processing in their minds the meaning of this procession but still followed Jonathan's band at a safe distance. When they arrived and the gate, they found it locked and as they hesitated the hostile hoard gathered in a tight semicircle around them. As the enemy built up a mass confidence the semicircle tightened, and the Babylonian soldiers drew their swords from their scabbards. Jonathan turned to face the threat, drew his Jericho 941 from his waist band, and with one burst of fire aimed above their heads had them flying in different directions. He then turned towards the locked gate and let off another burst of fire aimed at the massive padlock and its chain. The whole contraption together with a good chunk of the doors, exploded in all directions and the door flew open.

Facing them was an inner wall leading to the entry further along to the south of where they stood. Jonathan immediately recognised this as a dog-leg structure that gave the defenders the chance to shower the invaders with boiling oil from behind the screen facing them. He then turned to his followers to shout out that they were Israelite legionnaires bringing salvation to the Ark of the Covenant. As they finally entered the compound, they were surrounded by their brethren, who all paid tribute to their heavenly saviour by kneeling and repeating the *Shema* prayer. They then sent off a messenger to call to the *Cohen Hagadol,* the high priest, to welcome the angel and guide him to the Holy of Holies, where the Ark of the Covenant was to be found.

Whilst they waited, Jonathan and his band were offered wine and bread. They didn't have to wait long before a grey bearded, white-gowned important looking old gentleman appeared, wearing a complex breastplate and an elaborate turban covering his long grey hair.

He clearly was no fool and looked at Jonathan with a degree of scepticism. Speaking like a professional orator with a booming voice and a modest obeisance, he challenged the newcomer. "My people advise me that you are an angel and a messenger from Jehovah Hashem. I see your flaming sword and your bright halo, but our history tells us that the magicians of the pharaohs could perform clever tricks of all kinds. Can you prove that you are indeed God's messenger?" There was a sudden hush as Jonathan thought rapidly how to respond and tried the old Jewish trick of *schmoozing* the questioner and then answering a question with a question.

"My esteemed *Cohen Hagadol,* you question my authenticity as I expected and with this you also demonstrated your wisdom. Before I answer your question, you must answer my question to justify that you are worthy of your title. How many items are hidden in the Ark of the Covenant?"

The high priest answered instantly, "The Ark only contains the two tablets of Moses' ten commandments. What a stupid question, clearly you are a fraud."

"But you are wrong, high priest, there is a third item. Aaron's rod bearing a small branch with leaves. If you doubt it go and see for yourself."

"But I'm only allowed to enter the Holy of Holies on Yom Kippur, lest I die," wailed the high priest.

"You will be killed by the Babylonians along with the destruction of the temple together with the Ark, in any case, if you don't follow my instructions, so what have you got to lose?" responded Jonathan.

"All right then, this is what we do," conceded the Cohen Hagadol. "We will all visit the temple. I will bathe in the *Mikveh,* dress in fresh white clothes, say the secret prayers inside the Holy of Holies and then lift the angels off the golden ark and see how many items are hidden there. If, as you say, Aaron's rod is there, you must take the Ark and its contents to hide in a cave on Mount Nebo from where Moses saw the promised land." Everyone nodded agreement and a growing crowd of Israelites followed the high priest and the putative Angel of Hashem up the fifteen steps to the entrance of King Solomon's temple.

They then entered under the porch held up by the two bronze pillars, Jachin, and Boaz.

The porch led to the sanctuary that contained a candelabrum, a table, and a gold-covered altar used for offerings. In the sanctuary, loaves of Showbread were left as an offering to God. At the far end of the sanctuary there was a wooden door, guarded by two cherubim, leading to the Holy of Holies. Chains of gold further marked it off from the Holy of Holies. The floor of the temple was overlaid with gold. The doors of the Holy of Holies were of olivewood. On both sets of doors were carved cherubim, palm trees, and flowers, all being overlaid with gold. At each side were golden candelabra with branches for seven candles.

The interior of the Holy of Holies was a secret known only by the priesthood or Cohanim.

At this point, lined with the golden chain, the whole party knelt, apart from their alleged archangel. The high priest slipped through curtains on the left side of the entrance to home of the Ark to conduct his cleansing in the holy *Mikvah* with its seven steps one for each day.

He then returned fully covered in clean white linen robes from head to toe.

He then opened the door to Holy of Holies and for a short moment the audience could note the red mist of the *Nair Kodesh,* never ending light, seen through the smoke of the incense sticks. With the doors closed no one could hear the ardent prayers of the Cohen Hagadol, but within a few minutes the matter had been decided. The high priest exited the *Kadesh Hakodeshim* (קֹדֶשׁ הַקֳּדָשִׁים) holding himself upright with a fierce light shining from his eyes and announced, "The Angel of Hashem speaks the truth, and I therefore endorse his proposals. I need four legionnaires to follow me into the *Mikvah,* change into clean white robes, and then to follow me to where the Ark of the Covenant lies. They will then thread the carrying rods through the golden loops on the side of the casket bearing the golden angels and carry the sacred burden down to follow the guidance of the angel with the flaming torch." Jonathan was relieved as the batteries lighting the "flames" were running down.

And so it came to pass that the Ark of the Covenant ended up in a cave on the peak of Mount Nebo to await the building of the second temple by King Herod the Great.

# Chapter 11

## Masada 9th Av, 73 CE

Jonathan was feeling better with fewer panic attacks and good nights of dreamless sleep. He conjectured that his "time travel" prescribed by Dr Adler was starting to work. His wife, children, and grandchildren noticed the difference, but he would not share with them any details of his "psychotherapy". At his next visit to his therapist, he felt confident enough to question the need for more sessions. Dr Adler's response was both interesting and alarming. "I'm not surprised you're feeling better because you helped to heal one of the fractures of your timeline by rescuing the Ark of the Covenant that allowed the history of your people to continue to flow. Many others of the faith will attend to other fractures in due course. To secure your recovery you have two further tasks. The next is to save a life of one of your distant relatives, a progenitor of your family tree. For this visit to the past, you will need to wear a thoub of brown wool and wear sandals on your feet. You will also carry with you a book with blank pages and a clutch of HB pencils and this iron rod. If asked, claim your name is Flavius Josephus and that you are a scribe recording the history of the Israelites in their war against the Romans at the request of the high priest of the Pharisees, Aaron ben Ysacha HaCohen."

***

Jonathan prepared himself as required and walked through the molten glass at the back of Dr Adler's *aron kodesh* with confidence finding once more a platform with a familiar view. A thousand feet below was the hourglass shape of the Dead Sea, in the distance were the highlands of Jordan, misty in the rising heat of the lowest point of the earth. Somewhere amongst those distant peaks was Mount Nebo. However, what was of greatest interest were the differences he noted since he last stood there. He knew that he was standing on the eastern lip of the Masada plateau. In 1963 he was one of the volunteers recruited by Professor Yigal Yadin. He was given the task to lead a team of five to excavate the gaps between the double curtain defence walls built by King Herod in about 150 BCE. In the years 70–73CE, Zealots escaping from the capture of Jerusalem by the Romans established this last encampment of resistance on the ruins of Herod's winter palace, using the gaps between the curtain walls as hovels for their families to live. Every morning for the month of March 1963, Jonathan climbed up the Roman siege ramp from the volunteer's tent village to witness the dramatic sunrise behind the Jordanian mountain range, before getting to work on the back breaking archaeological dig. This involved pickaxing the stones and gravel from the walls that had collapsed inwardly, shovelling the debris into sieves, searching for any ancient artefacts, and throwing the rubble over the side 1,400 feet down to the accumulating pile at the base of Masada. This way they discovered ostraca, fragments of pottery carrying writing in primitive Hebrew letters, bronze coins, and rare intact examples of Roman glass. He considered this period of his life seminal and persuaded him to consider *aliyah* once he had completed his doctoral thesis. The view from where he was standing brought tears to his eyes before he had come to terms with the subtle differences in the view since his last visit. He was standing at the top of the snake path, the secret route leading up from the shores of the Dead Sea to the top of the plateau. It was the only way of climbing up the eastern wall of the rock face. It was a hazardous path with room for only one at a time. Even if the Romans found the entry, they could easily be picked off one at a time by dropping rocks on their heads. From where he stood the path looked in good shape. The first thing he noticed was that the Dead Sea was much wider than he remembered, with the water almost lapping at the base of the plateau. His memory was of 200 metres of salt flats to reach the water. The second anomaly was the growth of the Roman siege walls. In the 1960s they were to be made out with difficulty, no more than two rocks high, but now they reached the shoulders of the legionnaires patrolling alongside in pairs. Also, he could make out lookout towers every 100 metres with a Roman soldier standing with a long spear in his hand. It almost looked like a panorama from the film *Quo Vadis*. His ruminations were then interrupted by a woman's voice behind his back. "Who, by Jove, are you and where did you come from?"

Caught off guard he almost fell off the cliff. He spun round to find a beautiful young woman carrying a baby in tight swaddling in her arms. Not only was he taken by surprise he was speechless by the beauty of the stranger. She was tall and slim with eyes like sparkling emeralds, generous lips, and high cheekbones. Most of her hair was covered with a hood protecting her from the blistering sun above, but wisps of braided gold had escaped to provide a frame around her comely face. In no way did she appear like the prototype of a Jewish maiden but reminded him of Simonetta Vespucci, Botticelli's model for *The Birth of Venus*. Having digested that much he then noted the spark of intelligence in her eyes. They twinkled along with the hint of a smile. She then burst out laughing and said, "Old man close your mouth or you'll catch a fly, you look like one of our carp fishes with your dropped jaw."

Jonathan felt his blush rising up from his chest to his cheeks and coughed to cover his embarrassment. "Young lady, you took me by surprise, and I nearly fell to my death. My name Flavius Josephus and I am a scribe recording the history of the Israelites in their war against the Romans at the request of the high priest of the Pharisees, Aaron ben Ysacha HaCohen. I've just climbed up the snake path wearing my cloak of invisibility a gift from the miracles of Aaron's rod. As well as a scribe I am a magician and was present when we saved the Ark of the Covenant from the Babylonians 500 years ago. And who, beautiful maiden, might you be?"

The young lady could no longer control her mirth and burst out laughing, once she'd caught her breath she replied, "My name is Yehudit Bat Eliezer, HaCohen, and I don't believe a word you've said. Before I throw you over this mountain or fetch my husband to cut your throat, I will take you to see the head man of this colony of Zealots, Eleazer ben Yair. Just follow me."

As she led Jonathan to the northern tip of the plateau, he was amazed to see that the community was not a haphazard outpost but a perfectly organised village. The southern and central sections of the plateau were given over to fruit and vegetable gardens neatly squared off and free of weeds. Some of the fruit trees were tall enough to provide shade beneath which some villagers, if that was what he could call them, were taking a midmorning break. Clearly this had been the work of King Herod's labourers many decades in the past. He passed fishponds and saw a large carp buck angrily as it was netted up out of its refuge. He saw chicken roosts and goat pens with enough livestock to provide an endless supply of milk and eggs for the community. A lean-to shed hard against the eastern inner perimeter wall displayed barrels of wine while running right across his path as he walked northward were huge storage sheds whose open doors revealed open bags of corn, nuts, and dried fruit.

Along the way he also recognised a dairy with cream cheeses drying in muslin tubes hanging from the rafters, a laundry with bubbling cauldrons of water, and hard against the western wall the flames and sparks of a foundry's roaring fire. Everyone was bustling about his or her business with much laughter and shouting. There was a small market where housewives were bartering or trading with copper and silver coins. In among all this action, young children ran around unchecked, playing the games of village children anywhere in the land of Israel. To add to the sense of normality, close to the converted storeroom that housed their leader Eleazar ben Yair, he could hear the chanting of young male voices from a squat freestanding building that must have been a house of study; beyond it was a larger building that looked like a house of prayer. The largest and most impressive building stood against the western wall, a long way behind him, raised three stories high. He thought this was a king's palace and later was to learn that Herod and his family had lived there over sixty years ago but that now it was derelict and out of bounds.

The apparent sense of normality was not to last for long as he was brought into the presence of the great leader himself. It took a while for his eyes to adjust to the gloom of the unlit interior of the humble living quarters of the ben Yair family. Eleazar was sitting with a young child, maybe a year or so, gurgling happily on his lap. Eleazar was an imposing man wearing a small circular yarmulke, made of brightly patterned wool on the back of his head. His long ringlets and a long beard that appeared as black as pitch almost hid his face. His deeply set black eyes were full of foreboding but when he smiled at his visitor his brilliant white teeth lit up his face like shutters opening on a bright morning sky. He then turned to Yehudit and asked her to introduce the old man. With a bow of respect, she then recounted her story of her meeting with a wizard with the cloak of invisibility. This was said with a "tongue in her cheek" and a twinkle in her eyes that had bin Yair in a fit of laughter. Once he stopped laughing, he turned to face Jonathan with a fierce frown and demanded an explanation for his sudden appearance. Jonathan then suddenly realised that any explanation he could make up would remain unbelievable, so he thought he might as well tell the full truth and think of some evidence he might offer to convince the leader of the Zealots. A notebook and pencils might impress but not enough but describing an event or discovery from his time as a volunteer for Professor Yadin's excavations might win some trust. But before he started his discourse, he requested a cup of water and a cushion to sit down face to face with his inquisitor. Cross legged at face level with Eleazar ben Yair, refreshed by chilled water dragged up from one of the huge cisterns in the heart of the rock, he began to tell his story.

"My Lord, I am a humble man endowed with remarkable gifts awarded by Hashem. Listen to what I say and what I show you before dismissing me as a fraud. I have the gift of travelling through time and space, as a messenger and a scribe recording the history of our people. I have witnessed the destruction of the Temple of Solomon 600 years ago and the destruction of the second temple only three years ago. I witnessed the building of King Herod's Palace on Masada and revisited this place from a land thousands of thousands of cubits from the far north 2,000 years in the future. I see the future as well as I see the past and come to you with the greatest of respect, to warn you of horrors short to come. I arrived here not by climbing up the snake path wearing a cloak of invisibility but via a sacred route through the doors of an *aron kodesh*, the cabinet holding the five books of Moses."

He paused to drink from the cup of water and couldn't help noticing ben Yair exchanging glances with the Yehudit Cohen and was amused to see the beautiful young woman wiggling the index finger of her right hand around her temple bone. A symbol that was still in use in the 21st century. By this time Jonathan had remembered two findings from the excavation of Masada in 1963 that would be unknown to his host. "Come with me and I will show you proofs of my clairvoyance." He then stood up and raised his hand pointing back to where he was first found near the head of the snake path. The leader of the Zealots and the young woman, who still carried her sleeping baby, followed him, smiling at each other. Jonathan stopped and started to count the doorway leading into the makeshift hovels between to the curtain walls along the east edge of the massif. At the seventh doorway that was covered with a hessian curtain he stopped and asked Yehudit to invite the occupants outside. Grumbling as she ducked from under the lintel of the doorway, an old lady crawled out with two young children who had been eating their midday meal with their grandmother. On seeing ben Yair, she bowed and squatted down. The hovel had one stone wall all around the rectangular space, with a curtain dividing the room in two. In the north-east corner of the room there was a hearth marked off by bricks made of sand and straw. There was a pot warming up on glowing timber with smoke running up the corner to be let out a primitive chimney, a simple hole in the hessian covering the roof.

Jonathan then gave Yehudit orders, "Remove that pot from the fire and then put out the fire with the water in this cup." She did so and for a short time the hovel was clouded in steam. "Now pull away the bricks." At that the old grandmother started screaming but was silenced by one look from her overlord. "Now, Yehudit, can you see a large cavity under the bricks?"

She nodded yes. "Put your hand in the cavity and pull up the bag hidden there."

Doing as ordered Yehudit's arm disappeared and then reappeared with a bulbous canvas sack. "Now open the sack and pour out its contents." Yehudit and her master gasped as a pile of bronze coins flooded to floor. The old lady broke down in tears and Yehudit knelt to comfort her with an arm round her shoulder. By this time her baby was screaming for a feed. She jumped back up and without any shame or embarrassment offered her left breast.

Jonathan then turned to ben Yair and said, "Now you know what I mean. I suggest we put the coins back in the sack, put the sack back where we found it, so it can be left in peace until I rediscover it in 2,000 years' time. Let the old lady keep her hoard and let us go to a much more important secret we discovered at that time."

With the map of the buildings on the plateau in his head, Jonathan led his two companions in a northwestern direction until they came to the synagogue that backed on the western wall. Along the way he collected a group of the denizens who were curious about the stranger, the most remarkable of whom was the identical twin of Yehudit, who was introduced as Esther. Yehudit whispered in her sister's ear, who turned to look at Jonathan with wide eyes. They arrived at the water gate, which opened on a steep set of stairs used to supply the northern palace built on three terraces. The upper and middle terraces contained planters full of multicoloured flowering shrubs, colonnades carrying retractable sunshades, marble floors, and marble benches to sit and admire the view of the cliff faces overlooking the west shore of the Dead Sea. The lower terrace had a full panoply of traditional ancient Roman baths. As far as the residents of Masada were concerned, that was as far as you could go. Ben Yair shrugged his shoulders and declaimed for the benefit of his followers. "Adonai Josephus, this as far as we can go, and unless there's something buried under the tiles of the baths, what have you come to show us?"

"If you have a little more patience, I will show you," replied Jonathan. "My rod holds the secret. It may look like wood, but it is made of steel and if you look carefully, you'll note it has a sharp ferrule. I will need the help of two of your strongest men for my next trick."

There was no shortage of volunteers, Jonathan selected two and guided them to the base of the stairs. With the sharp end of his rod, he scraped away the earth and weeds from around the large square flagstone that acted as the platform between the last stair and the entrance to the Roman bathhouse. He then drove the end of the rod in the centre of the south facing side of the square and urged the strong men to lift the flagstone. After much huffing and puffing the stone suddenly flew back as if it were on hinges, leaving a deep dark hole open to view. The sun was past its meridian but there was still enough sunlight to see halfway down the shaft as well as showing iron loops in the wall at intervals designed for climbing up or down the shaft. Ben Yair sent off for a flaming torch and had one of his men climb down and see what was at the bottom. He returned after twenty minutes, sweating and breathless claiming that the shaft was long enough to reach the base of the massif. At the bottom he found an old grinding stone that looked as if it could be wheeled to hide or open an aperture large enough for a standing man to pass. This was clearly a secret escape route designed by King Herod the Great in the unlikely event of a siege of his winter palace. At the same time, it could enable escape for the present occupiers who were facing the unrelenting siege of the Roman army.

Ben Yair was truly impressed and turned to his strange visitor, bowing from the waist, and saying, "I am truly impressed and believe everything you told me, but please sir, who are you in all truth?"

To which Jonathan replied, "In truth I am as I said, a traveller from a land a long way away both in time and place, but I haven't yet explained the reason for my visit. I am indeed a servant of Hashem, and I am also a scribe required to record events that are soon to follow. I also have been given the task to save all the women and children imprisoned on Masada to carry the blood of all the fighters who will hold off the Seventh Legion of Augustus Silva whilst I plan their escape. You will go down in history as a band of Israelite warriors who were the greatest heroes of this époque. We will face this existential decision once the

Romans have built a siege tower that will overcome your defence.

***

As an involuntary time-traveller, Jonathan had no idea of the rules and consequences governing his time in times past. Was he using up his natural lifetime the longer he stayed away or were all his adventures, like dreams, the phantoms of one night? So far, he departed and returned to his natural time zone in what appeared to be one hour's therapy in Dr Adler's sitting room. Besides, his family might worry if he failed to turn up for dinner. He was now beginning to regret the implicit promise to people living on Masada, that he would hang around until the Romans had built something that would reach across the vertical gap of about 1,000 feet. Furthermore, he had to confess that he had no control of the matter as his adventures were entirely in the hands of his kabbalistic therapist. In the end and in the words of his grandchildren he would "go with the flow". The first hint of the "flow" was the appearance of Eleazer ben Yair's wife, Devorah, a handsome woman in her fifties, who reminded him of Shoshana his wife, introduced herself, and invited him for dinner and a bed in their spare chamber.

He soon settled into the bucolic lifestyle of the folk living on the plateau of Masada. He was even giving the tasks of cleaning the fish-pools teaching maths and reading at the school for children aged seven to eleven. The practices of Judaism were very similar with that he grew up in London but with some curious discrepancies. The most obvious was that chicken was not considered meat and could be eaten along with dairy products. There were no large bovine sources of meat, but they kept a herd of goats who provided milk and meat. Their hind legs were hobbled to prevent them jumping to their death over the side of the curtain walls to join the ghost of the scapegoats. It took a while to realise that amongst the Israelites there were dark-skinned Nubian women who were active as slaves. This became obvious the

69

first Sabbath he was there. To avoid the housewives breaking the laws of working on *Shabbat* the Nubian girls attended to the fires and the cooking.

The synagogue on the western wall was built on two levels with a lectern on a *bimah* in the centre. The ground floor was for the men who could sit on benches around the perimeter or crossed legged on cushions in a circle round the *bimah.* The women were all hidden behind a perforated wooden screen in a balcony on the upper floor reached by stairs on the outside. The service in the synagogue was remarkably like that in Highgate or Hampstead Garden Suburb. The obvious difference was that they directed their prayers to the west towards the ruins of the second temple instead of directing your prayers to Jerusalem in the east of London NW3. There was a reading portions from the *Sefer Torah* (the five books of Moses) written on lamb skin velum rather than a scroll of the best parchment. They even had a prayer for the royal family, not the house of Windsor but the decedents of the house of King David. The services were conducted by members of the family of the erstwhile high priest. They formed a tribe called the *Cohanim* they considered themselves princely and were notorious for their long sermons that could last an hour at a time when the outside temperature was in the high thirties. The women had the advantage of creeping away unseen. The men who stayed the course were a least rewarded with a *kiddush* under a canopy outside the synagogue where a goblet of the finest wine was blessed and passed around the congregation. Each man had his on goblet in his tunic pouch to try out the other wines on the table as comely Nubian girls passed round platters bearing fruit and sweet delicacies.

***

After six months of siege, it became apparent that the Romans had become bored of this waiting game and had determined on another stratagem to break the will of Masada. One Shabbat when the day was at its longest and the heat at its highest, while all the population on the plateau were at their devotions on their day of rest, something changed.

The Romans had cleverly chosen that day to prepare for the building of a structure that would carry them up to the level of the walls on the western side of Masada. On Yom Rishon, the day after the Sabbath, they awoke to the cries of their lookouts, who pointed below. While their minds were on other things the Romans had breached their own siege wall and transported a huge load of timbers and building materials and laid them out in readiness for the building of a siege ramp. Such an undertaking appeared superhuman.

As soon as the people above understood the Romans' plan, they responded with sling shots, arrows, and any missile that came to hand. At this distance their efforts were puny and barely slowed the Romans in their work, especially as their slaves took the brunt of their best efforts and clearly, they were considered disposable – there were plentiful replacements among the defendants' poor brethren transported in cages from Judea.

After a few days observing their method, Jonathan was able to deduce their plan, making use of his knowledge of trigonometry, produced some simple drawings, and took them to our council of elders. This way he was able to convince Eleazar ben Yair of the Roman's improbable plan and that they could no longer passively wait for them to abandon their siege. As judged by the shape and size of the base of their structure built out of massive tree trunks, he was able to deduce the size and inclination of a pyramidal dais that would eventually climb to the foot of their fortifications on the western wall, aiming a little to the south of their house of prayer. Day by day they witnessed the structure grow and marvelled at the ingenuity of the Roman engineers. They appeared to be building a ziggurat like those of the ancients of Babylon, except at each step they covered the wooden frame with boulders and earth. And so, the ramp grew day by day. After a few months they were within reach of the

Zealot's missiles and began to take heavy loses. This certainly slowed them down, but on each Shabbat their foolish leaders insisted that everyone refrain from work and warfare and these lulls, of course, were exploited as the Roman workers doubled their efforts – and the ramp grew at a slow but relentless pace.

After two months, when once again the Romans were given a free hand as the Judean men of war bowed down in prayer to the almighty at Rosh Hoshana and Yom Kippur, it became apparent that the Lord had abandoned them to their fate and the new platform on the siege tower allowed the Roman archers a good footing to pour down fire as their flaming arrows arched overhead. Toward the end of Succoth, it was obvious to all, save those who had kept faith with their fickle and petulant God, that they were doomed.

About this time Jonathan was summoned to meet with the council of elders and their leader. Looking gaunt and exhausted, ben Yair outlined his dreadful plan. They were surrounded by the whole population on the plateau. Rather than be taken alive, all but himself, those living on Masada, would die. Each father would kill his wife and children and then those left would draw lots to determine the order in which they killed one another. As for their prophet and scribe, he would be allowed to escape and pass on the story of Masada for two thousand years or more. Jonathan was appalled at this barbaric solution and came up with a more humane suggestion.

"My dear friends, I have lived with you for six months and love you all like my own family. I admire your courage but be inspired by the words of Hashem, 'the loss of one life is like the loss of the whole world'. Suicide or patricide is a sin. The Lord has indeed appeared to have left you in this invidious situation but look upon this as a test. Let me relay the words of the Lord as I dreamt last night. All fit fighting men from the age of eighteen to the age of fifty should indeed fight to the bitter end, holding off the Romans whilst the others make their escape." At that point there was an uproar. First it appeared that all the elderly men felt humiliated, they too wanted to fight to their death, as in any case their length of life was short. Next to join in the row to the amazement of Jonathan, was Devorah, the wife of their leader.

"Oh, prophet from your distant land, you insult the women of the Israelite tribes. We can fight as well as our menfolk when it's a matter of life or death. You may note that some of our husbands have swollen bruises round their eyes." All the women present laughed and applauded, nodding to each other in agreement. "We will fight alongside our men when the Romans might not expect it. We will use our red-hot steering spoons and the long needles we use for making our lamb skin curtains. And finally, we have sharp teeth and know to bite in the neck to draw the most blood." Once again there was cheering from the women, until it came to a sudden stop as a bent old woman who looked like a witch raised her stick and screamed two words in an unknown language. Maybe she *was* a Jewish witch. The witch then spoke out words of wisdom with a strange accent that sounded almost Mancunium.

"Listen to me, my dear womenfolk. Remember that men are clever and strong but don't forget that women are wise and brave. Men will never experience the pain of giving birth. Can there be a worse pain when fighting with the Roman oafs? Let us compromise. All women who are pregnant or lactating must be saved. All girls under the age of bat mitzvah can choose to fight or not. All other women from the age of eighteen to my age, 110, should support the men in cunning ways, bringing their swords out from between their breasts and laying booby traps."

The plan that was finally accepted was as follows: The women with their young children under the age of thirteen, the women who were lactating or pregnant, and their Nubian maidservants, would hide with adequate supplies in one of the labyrinthine channels of the water cisterns inside the great rock. Entrances to these cisterns were well hidden thanks to the ingenuity of King Herod's architects. They were to stay hidden until the Romans had cleared the site, as it was assumed they wouldn't stay long once the resistance had been crushed. The major northern cistern had been built to supply water to King Herod's palace at the northern tip of our fortress. The hidden water gate near the bathhouses where slaves could carry jars of water down through a hidden niche in the western rock face to the lower terraces would allow for them to escape unseen. From the lowermost terrace there was a drop of about eighty metres as uncovered by Jonathan. Escape from this side of Masada would be considered impossible and therefore would not be watched. They would be led by Jonathan, and his strength and the use of his rod as a crowbar would be sufficient to roll away the rock closing the exit.

On the 9th of Av, precisely three years after the fall of the second temple, the Roman legionnaires completed their ramp and siege tower and broke through the western walls of Masada. Hopelessly outnumbered, the defenders of the plateau, both the fighters of the Zealots and Sicarii detachments, battled for nearly a day until all the men were dead and many of the fighting women were shackled and taken as slaves. After another twelve hours whilst the Roman soldiers searched every upstanding structure for hidden Jews, followed by a bacchanalia of eating and drinking followed by the rape of the youngest slaves, they made their way back to their camp at the northwest margin of the rock walls of the Masada massif.

The following day the Roman legion marched away along the hazardous wadi Masada running to the southwest that would ultimately take them to Beersheba and then back to Rome carrying the Golden Menorah from the sacked temple.

***

Once the coast was clear, the women, children, and handmaidens, guided by Jonathan, walked due north, keeping close to the edge of the ramparts facing the Dead Sea and carrying enough water and food for at least two days. At daybreak on the 12th of Av, they were met by a band of Sicarii who had been based at an outpost in Qumran at the northernmost limit of the Dead Sea. They has been summoned by pigeon post and were to provide mules to carry their modest loads as well as supply them with food and water. They were then guided to a cave in wadi Ein Gedi, a day's walk to the north, where the refugees were to lay hidden until it was known that the Dead Sea valley was free of Roman legionnaires.

Some chose to travel north to the hills of north of the *Kineret,* the Sea of Galilee, and when reached and given sanctuary by a small Jewish community they chose to sojourn there and built a small temple that exists to this day known as the Zenati Synagogue.

Others chose to turn south with their mules and made their way to the southern tip of the Dead Sea and then turned west toward Beersheba. From there they joined a caravan disguised as one of the spice traders *enroute* to Akaba and then carry on by sea to the spice lands of the Indies. After six months they reached a safe haven among the dark-skinned people who had traded with Judah since the times of King Solomon.

Jonathan had elected to follow the group of women to the north where one gave birth to a little boy, who Nathan Adler assured Jonathan was an antecedent of the male line of his family.

# Chapter 12

## Jehudah Halevi and the Crusades

When Jonathan rejoined the world of actuality, he was surprised to learn that his prolonged absence on Masada accounted for a mere 55minutes on the clock in Dr Adler's clock in his consulting lounge. He was now getting used to the pliable or elastic nature of time, one step nearer to the understanding Einstein's theory of relativity. He felt exhausted but jubilant to have identified the antecedent of the male line of his family. A week later he was alarmed that he was now expected to return the compliment by discovering the location of the grave of the most important antecedent of the male line for Dr Adler. This is how the story went.

"In December 1066, the head of the Jewish community in Granada was assassinated and the whole community were assaulted by a ravenous mob of Moslems who claimed the lives of 4,000 Jews. 20 years later, at a time when Jews and Muslims had made peace with each other, an adolescent Yehudah Halevi, made the long journey from his hometown in Tudela to Granada. He was an ambitious poet and wanted to have the guidance of Moishe ibn Ezra, the most celebrated poet of his period. Very soon the young Halevi outplayed his master and was invited to Seville to support the difficult life of the Jewish community by writing divine poetry to embellish weddings and funerals. He was then persuaded to move on to Toledo and retained as a doctor; something relatively achieved in those days. Despite of that two of his three children died, leaving him despondent for the rest of his life. This is reflected by one of his most famous rhymes:

All my desire is here before you

whether or not I speak of it
I'd seek your favour for an instant then die
if only you would grant my wish
I'd place my spirit in your hand
then sleep and in that sleep find sweetness.


He wandered round the middle east and once celebrated Passover in Cairo. He then chose to spend the rest of his life in the promised land. He the boarded a ship Alexandria sailing to Acre and from there he had planned to settle in Jerusalem. Assuming he survived that relatively short voyage he should have arrived in late May or early June 1096. That coincided with the first crusade to Jerusalem. Nothing more is learnt of him, but a document discovered in the Cairo genizah suggests the child who survived was the important antecedent of *my* male line. Your task, Johnathan, is to time shift to 1096 and trace the last travels of Yehuda Halevi. Did he reach Acre and was he buried in Jerusalem. You will have to wear clothing of a Benedictine Monk, a black tunic, cowl, scapular, shoes, and sandals. Wear a cross around your neck, because if a Crusader knight thinks you are Jewish, he might chop off your head, but if he assumes you are a Monk of that order, you will be treated with respect."

Jonathan was familiar with Acre; it had the most famous fish restaurant in Acre Israel called Uri Buri after the name of its charismatic bearded owner. It's renowned for its fresh, seasonal seafood, that included shellfish considered non-kosher by orthodox Jews. He had also visited the awesome Templar fortress built by the Crusaders to protect the harbor and had walked through the tunnel 150 meters long and it extends from the Templars fortress in the west to the city's port in the east.

The Templars were a military-monastic order who – in the name of the Pope Urban II– aided pilgrims coming from Europe to visit the holy sites of the Land of Israel. From

Acre many settled in Jerusalem, on the Temple Mount, hence their name, "the Templars", the guardians of the Temple. What Dr Adler went on to say was alarming.

"My dear Jonathan, please forget everything you learnt about the crusaders at school and forget the patron Saint of England, St George and his dragon. You probably were taught that they were noble and chivalrous Christian Knights, wearing chain mail and wearing a white tabard bearing a red cross, carrying a lance and bearing a shield with a red cross as well. They were nothing like that. The first Crusade was entirely Franks, mostly from a region we now call France. They were followed by a crowd of ignorant unemployed thugs, camp followers and prostitutes. On the way to Constantinople, they wiped out any Jewish community they encountered and then crossing Byzantium to the near East, they murdered any Arabs and Muslims that stood in their way.

To find Yehudah Halevi you first have to find Moishe ibn Ezra in Acre to see if he made the crossing from Alexandria. Paradoxically In the 11th century, Acre was a thriving port city with a notable Jewish community. During the Crusader period, Acre became a major commercial centre, attracting Jewish immigrants, including scholars from Europe. Before the Crusaders made their attempt at taking Jerusalem, they needed to reequip their armament and replace their exhausted horses. Like it or not, most of the traders were Jewish and they were beholden to them. The Jews acted as armorers trading iron armour, shields, and leatherworkers trading leather armour, including leather horse armour. If ibn Ezra remembers him and claims Halevi made it to Jerusalem, you then have to follow the crusaders in their pilgrimage.

In the 11th century, Jerusalem's Jewish community was relatively small and faced various challenges, including periods of instability and conflict. While the city was under Muslim rule, Jewish life continued, with communities centred around synagogues and engaging in religious and economic activities. However, the arrival of the Crusaders in the late 11th century brought significant upheaval, including violence and displacement of the Jewish population. You will arrive at Jerusalem at the very time that the first Crusade surrounds the walls and holds the old city in a siege before breaking through at the Jaffa gate at 1099 CE just like the British army in 1917. Your role is to find Yehuda Halevi either alive or in his grave, before the Crusaders break in."

Having clothed himself like a monk, hiring the costume from a shop in Camden Town, he returned to Dr Adler's time traveller and in the blink of an eye found himself in a massive bastion, at least 30 feet high and all built with huge granite rocks, covered with pennants representing the coat of arms of each of the princely lines supplying the leaders of the first Crusade. He recognised it immediately as the interior of the Crusader castle towering over the southwest boundary of Acre overlooking the Mediterranean, last seen as a sightseer on his last trip to Israel. A small group of Crusader knights were sitting in a corner drinking beer from pewter tankards. They looked up with alarm when Jonthan suddenly appeared but were sufficiently drunk not to worry about a Benedictine monk rising out from the floor. After all these monks were deeply involved in the political and social landscape of the time, influencing the spread of Crusader ideology and providing support for crusading expeditions. Knowing his way to the secret tunnel whose entry was covered by the banner of the Maltese Cross, white on a red field, he slipped under the drape and walked slowly south, with Crusader families walking in the opposite direction ignoring him. Once in the open air in the busy centre of old Acre he started to look for the Jewish quarter.

This was a problem. Acre was on the northern tip of the long crescent bay ending at Jaffa, and that's where he will need to be, to start his journey to the hills bearing the holy city of Jerusalem. The tunnel he just passed through passed underneath the town, but he was not sure in which direction. He needed to find his way to the harbour once he'd found the Jewish quarter, but he stood at a junction of five different alleyways overlooked by blocks four or five floors. He had not memory of the place from his visit as a tourist. He would have to ask the way from strangers who might look Jewish but then they might ignore or run from a man dressed like a Benedictine monk. But then as if on cue, a scene was acted out by two men that might have come from Shakespeare's Shylock. In the centre of this little square at the junction of the five alleyways an argument was building up between two elderly men.

One was aristocratic in his dress and demeanour, and the other was bent over with a hunchback, wearing black robes down to the floor, but also wearing a black skull cap with long peyot dangling in front of his ears. He had found his Jew and couldn't but assume that the bent old man was asking for his loan to be returned. Some coins were exchanged and the haughtily man strode off with disgust graven on his face. Jonathan then walked across to the old Jew and greeted him with the traditional Hebrew words, *Shalom aleichem,* meaning Peace unto you. The old man had a fright being greeted by a monk looking sinister under his hood. To calm him down he tried talking to him in *Ivrit,* modern Hebrew which he had mastered on his many visits to Israel to deliver his lectures. It had the wrong effect on the terrified money lender, who ran off down one of the alleys shouting, "Help, help, a Golem is chasing me!!". Jonathan followed his direction until he reached a *shtiebel*: a small, informal place for Jewish communal prayer, within what looked like any private home. It had a Magen David over the portico and posters written in Hebrew stuck all over the walls. Waiting him at the door were a group of white bearded men wearing black hats and holding cudgels. Jonathan rapidly dropped his hood and held his hands up to the sky using the universal gesture of "I come in peace without a weapon". Then in using remnants of his Hebrew education said, *"Ve gam an'ee Yehuda, an'ee hinay b'shalom,"* more or less saying, "I'm also Jewish I come in peace." Some of the bearded hostile men laughed at his English accent and the apparent leader of the group responded:

"I think we would understand your English better than your Hebrew but why should we believe you are a Jew when your dressed like a Benedictine monk?" To which Jonathan responded, *"Shema Yisrael Adanoi elahanoo Adanoi echod",* translated into English would be, "Listen Israelites, your God is the only one God." The leader of the gang with the biggest black hat and the longest white beard replied, "Any Christian monk could learn that line, prove you are a Jew by showing us your circumcision!'. Jonathan was in a state of shock and was about to hold up his robes, when all the white bearded men burst out laughing, and their leader flapped his hands and in tears of hilarity hollered, "No need, no need, we know you're a Jew because of your *Chutzpah. Nu?* So, what can we do for you"

"I am looking for Moishe ibn Ezra", said Jonathan.

"You have found him. I am Moishe ibn Ezra, so what can I do for you?"

"I'm told that you can lead me to Yehuda Halevi the poet."

"I am a poet." replied ibn Ezra, "Am I not good enough for you?"

"You are the greatest poet in the world, and I even remember some of your lines:

*The pining lover turns to an apple for succour*
*whose fragrance recalls your breath like myrrh*
*its shape is your breast*
*and it's the flush that races through your cheeks when*
*you blush.*

I'm looking for Yehuda Halevi for another reason", countered Jonathan.

Now it was Moishe ibn Ezra's instance to blush in delight at the compliment delivered by this mysterious stranger. Once he had recovered from his discomfiture, ibn Ezra continued his cross examination. "So, what is the reason for searching for my talented colleague and furthermore who on earth are you?" Jonathan had anticipated that question and prepared the answer having studied ibn Ezra's writings as a philosopher as well as a poet. "You ask who on earth am I, that is a good question but assumes I am a denizen of earth. Your essays on the relation between man and God are vivid and clear but you left out the probability that God might send messengers not of this earth that ignorant folk call angels. I can prove this by reading your mind. You believe that God's perfection cannot be comprehended by the human mind, and the finite and imperfect human mind cannot know the infinite and perfect mind of God. I come to you at this time and place having travelled 1,000 years in time and 1,000 leagues in space. There is a hazardous fissure in a nodule of time-space that can only be corrected if I can protect Yehuda Halevi from decapitated by a Crusader's sword." At that point, overcome with awe, ibn Ezra and his colleagues prostrated themselves at the feet of Jonathan and chanted the prayer, *"Blessed are You, LORD, our God, King of the Universe, who has imparted wisdom to those that fear You."*

On rising ibn Ezra took Jonathan's hand and walked with through a maze of backstreets until they reached the harbour. He then charted a hulk with a single sail to sail his guest close to the shore all the way to Jaffa. He then explained to Jonathan that all he knew about Halevi and his travels is that he was anticipating to take the short cut from Jaffa to Jerusalem ahead of the Crusader army, so that should he die in their battle to conquer the holy city, he might be buried on the Mount of Olives so that at the instance of resurrection, when the Messiah comes, he will be one of the first to go to heaven.

...............................

Jonathan cruise to Jaffa, sailing close to the beaches and coastlines and the docking at the small ancient harbour, were uneventful but when he started to look for the road from Jerusalem, he was disappointed. All he could find was a muddy footpath recording the previous pilgrims' determination to reach the Church of the Holy Sepulchre and the mount Golgotha upon which Jesus was crucified. The distance from Jaffa to Jerusalem was about 50 miles and trudging along this pathway up hill, would take him at least two days. When about halfway there, and as the sun was setting behind, he started looking for a spot to spend the night. Other pilgrims had passed this way, and a small inn was to be found nearby, that offered a bowl of gruel, and a straw filled paillasse for the night and a handful of dates and a cup of goat's milk for breakfast. As he restarted his journey dressed as a monk, he found himself a rod made from a fallen branch of a tree, to ease to walk that had become steeper.

Once close to the embattlements of the Holy city, he circumnavigated it to the south and entered the Kidron valley. He then started climbing again to the east until he was halfway up the Mount of Olives from where he had a bird's eye view of what was going on in and around the city below. He could see frenetic activity in the lower city where most of the Jew lived and the upper city that housed most of the Muslim Arabs. Coming from beneath the southern walls, were the legions of Crusaders in full armour, the knights walking alongside their stallions followed by the foot-soldiers carrying their long spears, they had yet to build their siege towers. One legion broke away and continued round to Mount Zion, the hill on the southern border of the city, allowing the fighting men a good view above the Hinnom valley, that allowed them to view of the battlements from a second side in order to have two lines of attack, the upper city defended by the Muslims and the lower city defended by the Jews.

In spite of the fact that the two hostile militias were beyond reach, the defenders standing on their parapets, were shooting flaming arrows in a futile way. Jonathan saw all that and realised he had only a short time to find and rescue Yehuda Halevi. He had one advantage over the Crusader legions that he had learnt as a sightseer two or three years ago. The battlements of the eastern side, built upon the highest hill, where of no interest to the enemy because they could never build a siege tower tall enough to drop a wooden flap to cross over the top. Yet had they known the one fault in the sanctuary, was in the valley below the Mount of Olives, as was known as Hezekiah's tunnel. It was a secret source of water built by King Hezekiah to supply water during a siege. It started in the Gihon spring in the Kidron valley and took a serpentine route underground and then under the foundations of the walls, ending up at the Pool of Siloam inside the southeast corner of the lower City. Only in the wet season was the tunnel impossible to walk through, but at this time of the year you could walk through with water up to your ankles. There was no time to waste before the Crusaders built their siege towers, so Jonathan with his rod, scampered down the hill and found the entry to the tunnel hidden behind a bush. Once he had walked and splashed his way about three meters inside the tunnel, he lit a candle from a matchstick from a box in his pouch and had no difficulty in walking through to the pool of Siloam. As he emerged from the water, a pretty young girl with a pitcher in the pool to collect water, had the fright of her life, screamed and ran away shouting: "There's a demon in the pool!". This drew a crowd of curious Jews. "Shalom Aleichem chaverim, I come in peace to carry out the command of *Hashem Adoni Elohaynoo*, I must see the poet Yehuda Halevi." One of the long-bearded men gawping at him, who seemed to be a member of authority, sent a young boy to fetch the poet. Time stood still until the well-travelled poet and prophet elbowed his way through the throng and amazed Jonathan with the words; "Professor Tannenbaum I assume." He continued, "What's more I'm aware of the reason for your visit, don't ask how because like you I have metaphysical skills that can't be explained. My travels from the Iberian peninsula, through Europe and then to the Holy land and Zion, have been a search for the *Shekhina,* the Divine presence. The fact that that Jerusalem will soon be in the hands of the Crusaders and the Jews will soon be massacred makes my vocation more nor less urgent. I listen to my inner voice that tells me where there are enough Jews standing on the Mount of Olives facing the Temple Mount, the *Shekhina* would return to the ruined shrine from which she has fled; and when she is manifest, the Messiah will reappear. Let us all leave this place and follow you through King Hezekiah's tunnel, cross the Kidron valley, climb the Mount of Olives, and face the Temple Mount. Whether the *Shekhina* returns or not, your task is done, and your name will be written in Hashem's book of the faithful, for ever and ever!" At that point the surrounding panorama became pixilated, and Jonathan felt himself flying backwards 1,000 years into the future.

......................................

# Chapter 13

## 1506: The Lisbon Massacre

Jonathan's return to Dr Adler's clinic was more dramatic than the past. He seemed to crash backwards through the glacial boundary between the first century CE into the present day. Even his therapist was alarmed by his manner of entry. This time he noted the clock had recorded one hour and ten minutes in his absence and clearly the window for his time travel had closed during his time abroad. Dr Adler apologized and claimed that this was the first time of a late return in his practice. He took it as a warning that his patient's aptitude for time travel was more than anyone else, he had treated, and to avoid the risk of Jonathan being locked in the past he would have to make some minor adjustments to his space/time rheostat. But at least on the positive side he had secured the paternal line of his genealogy.

***

The following week Dr Adler changed his routine in a spectacular manner. On opening the shell-like doors of the Ark, instead of a transparent window into the next episode to the lives of Jonathan's tribe, there was a spinning wheel of lines with numbers and words. More like a "one armed bandit" at Vegas than a window into the past. As the spinning slowed down, he could eventually capture the meaning of the numbers and words that described the dates for the high points and low points in the history of the Jews. It finally stopped at an episode he had never heard of.

*130 Hadrian, visiting Jerusalem, decides to rebuild it as a Roman city - an act which provokes the final Jewish uprising*

*135 After the Roman recovery of Jerusalem from Simon Bar-Kochba, all Jews are expelled from the city*

*300 The Jews of the Diaspora have by now spread through much of the Roman empire, where they are treated with tolerance*

*600 Ritual intoning of the psalms, derived from Jewish synagogues, is formalized in Christian worship as Gregorian chant*

*650 Jews and Christians, sharing with Muslims the status of 'people of the book', are promised religious tolerance in the Qur'an*

*800 The Jews prosper in the Muslim and Carolingian empires, forming strong communities in Spain and in Germany*

*921 The Jewish calendar, deriving originally from the example of Babylon, is given its lasting form*

*930 Saadiah Gaon writes a seminal work of Jewish philosophy in his Book of Beliefs and Opinions*

*1096 The German crusade begins with a massacre of Jews in many of the region's cities*

*1099 Crusaders capture the holy city of Jerusalem and massacre the Muslim and Jewish inhabitants*

*1180 In Cairo the Jewish philosopher Moses Maimonides writes, in Arabic, a much-translated text with the endearing title Guide to the Perplexed*

*1200 The new Christian doctrine of Transubstantiation prompts rumours that the Jews desecrate the consecrated Host*

*1290 The classical work of the Kabbalah, the Zohar, is almost certainly the work of the Spanish Kabbalist Moses de Leon.*

*The Jews in England are driven out of the country, soon to be followed by those in France*

*1348 Massacres of Jews, rumoured to have caused the Black Death by poisoning wells, begin in southern France and spread through much of Europe*

*1480 Tomas de Torquemada, from a family of converted Jews, is appointed Spain's first Grand Inquisitor*

*1492 Torquemada persuades Ferdinand and Isabella to expel from Spain all Jews, about 160,000, who would not convert to Christianity*

*1506 The Lisbon Massacre.*

The spinning list of catastrophes suddenly stopped leaving Jonathan speechless. Dr Adler broke the silence. "I suspect like most of our race; you have never heard of the Lisbon Massacre. And to tell the truth it is best forgotten. But in your case, it is critical, as once again you need to fine-tune a point in the time-space continuum that will defend the origin of your maternal line and all its branches. Let me tell you about this ugly pustule in the history of our people. This event illustrates the true meaning of genocide, a word that has been hijacked in modern times by the UN to demonize Israel."

At this point Jonathan interrupted, having been chewing over a paradox since the last the last appointment with his therapist.

"Dr Adler, with respect, I'm totally confused by an enigma that has perturbed me all week and can only get worse from what you about to tell me. My time travel last week concluded with my intervention that protected my paternal line. Now you're about to send me on a voyage through time again to protect my maternal line. Yet before I met you, I existed as a human being with warm memories of my mother and father. So, what was the need of these adventures to fine-tune my time-space field if I was already here, knocking on your door, seeking therapy to cure my bad dreams and panic attacks? Not only that, but I also have two generations, children and grandchildren, that prove my actuality."

"My dear Professor Tannenbaum," responded Dr Adler, "I wondered how long it might be before you asked that question. What you describe is known in my trade as the 'time bending paradox', let me try and explain. We all assume that we ride on the front edge of time into the darkness of the future. Yet a healthy mind needs a proper relationship with time, which is clearly not linear, but something more mysterious that can be experienced in many ways. Very few individuals recognise this phenomenon, and they tend to be those with the highest intelligence quota. The commonest example is known as déjà vu but this is also experienced as the aura before a migraine attack. Collective Unconscious is a theory that has been used to explain the phenomenon. Collective Unconscious is a controversial theory created by Carl Jung. His theory was that all people have a shared pool of knowledge that has been passed down through generations and we can unconsciously access this knowledge. For now, though, I ask you to trust me and in the fullness of time, no pun meant, you will understand why I send you on these travels through time.

"As I was saying, in the 1500s Portugal saw a new, virulent strain of the Black Death, which impacted Jews less than the Christians due to their better hygiene. This led to conspiracy theories, and Jews were blamed for causing the disease. The event that ignited the pogrom took place on Sunday, 19th April 1506, at the Church of São Domingos, when the congregation was praying for an end to plague and drought. During the mass, a light appeared to fix on a crucifix. Catholic believers interpreted it as a miracle, a supernatural revelation. News spread throughout Lisbon and people from across the city rushed to the church. But when a young Jew tried to explain that the light was just the reflection of a candle, the Christians were outraged. He was set upon and beaten, then dragged to a square, mutilated, and killed. The massacre then began. Large bonfires were lit along the banks of the Tagus River to which hundreds of mutilated bodies were transported. Jewish children were thrown into the bonfires alive. Even babies were flung into the flames as butchered bodies filled the city. Heads were borne aloft on the tips of lances. There were so many victims the pogromists wanted to burn that there wasn't enough firewood to fuel the city's pyres. More than 3,000 Jews of all ages would be killed on 19 to 21 April. The authorities tried to stop the butchery, but when the municipal magistrate, invested with royal authority, arrived to prevent more bloodshed, he was himself pursued and almost killed. There were acts of individual heroism by Christians. Some attempted to hide their Jewish neighbours. João Mascarenhas, the king's squire and holder of customs rights in Lisbon and Oporto, courageously faced the murderous mob, warning them of Portugal's decline as a global power if its Jewish community was destroyed. He was killed by the mob for his bravery. Your role is to stop that carnage. How? You will be inspired."

***

The moment Dr Adler stopped speaking, Jonathan felt himself flying through the window of time and landing in an alien setting witnessing horrors that had never been seen in liberal countries of the West for more than 300 years. It was early in the morning, and he was in the midst of a noisy crowd wearing a rough brown itchy habit with his head covered by a pointed hooded scapular, a beaded belt, and open sandals that exposed dirty toes and unkempt toenails. There were many dressed like that, so he made his way to the front of a noisy crowd unnoticed. He saw a semicircle of heavy wooden stakes standing up about six foot each with a mound of sticks and other flammable material at its base. The crowd fell silent when an old man wearing a black skull cap on the long sideburns, the markings of an orthodox

90

Jew, appeared from the direction of the city jail, led by a priest, followed by two men carrying the Jew between them on a wooden chair. They had to force their way through the crowd, who made way reluctantly as if they would have liked to obstruct the progress of the chair but did not quite have the courage. Women from the old Jew's family wailed piteously as the helpless man was tied upright to a wooden stake in the ground. He kept slipping down on his useless legs that clearly had been fractured by the tortures that had clearly pre-empted the *auto-de-fe*. His tormentors had to bind him tightly to keep him in place. The watchmen piled additional firewood around his legs whilst a bishop intoned a prayer in Latin. The chair carriers picked up the torches that had lit their night-time labours and waited for a signal from the bishop who stood in front of their victim. When he dropped his arm, the chair carriers put their torches to the firewood around the old Jew's legs. The dry wood caught quickly, and the flames crackled with hellish merriment. Their victim cried out feebly at the heat. Wood smoke choked the nearest watchers, who backed away. Soon there was another smell, one that was at once familiar and sickening, the smell of roasting meat. The old man began to scream in pain. In between screams he yelled: '*Shema Yisrael adonai elhhanu adonai echad*. Take me, Lord! Now, please, now!' But God did not take him yet. Jonathan had once read that merciful judges sometimes allowed the family to hang a bag of gunpowder around the neck of the condemned man so that his end would be quick. But this inquisitor evidently had not permitted that kindness. The lower half of the body burned while the victim remained alive. The noise he made in his agony was unbearable to hear, more like the squealing of a terrified animal than the sound of a man. At last, he fell silent; perhaps the smoke suffocated him; perhaps the heat boiled his brain. The fire continued to burn, and the dead body of the Jew turned into a blackened ruin. The smell was disgusting, but at least the noise had stopped. Jonathan thanked God it was over at last. He had never seen anything so dreadful. He did not know how men could do such things and did not understand why God would let them. When the spectators began to drift away from this pyre to the next in line, Jonathan remained. The sun rose, though it did not shine on the smouldering remains, which remained in the cold shadow of the nearby Basilica of Saint Francis of Assisi. He was at a loss on how to delay or negate the continued torture and slaughter of his people whilst dressed like a Franciscan friar. It needed a miracle, and he found himself praying the *Shema,* the last words of the scorched victim. He found himself walking absent minded into the portico of the basilica and drawn towards the pulpit. He climbed up the wooden spiral stairs as if he was about to deliver a sermon to an absence of a congregation. After all the noise he witnessed outside, he found the absolute silence of the cathedral comforting. Suddenly the silence was interrupted by the sound of rain drops coming from on high. He turned round and lifted his head to meet the gaze of a beautiful ceramic statue of a young woman draped in a blue gown. The raindrops were coming from her eyes, but they were not tears, they were drops of blood. Clearly the young woman was an effigy celebrated by Roman Catholics as Mary the mother of Jesus. When he had prayed for a miracle, this was the last thing he expected, but as there were many miracles in the Old Testament, a new one from the New Testament was just as welcome as long as it was good for the Jews. A bell rope hung within his reach and with a hefty pull it gratifyingly responded with a high-pitched ding-dong. He pulled and pulled and pulled, until an assembly of monks of his cult came running in to see who had defiled the basilica. When they were within reach of his voice, Jonathan shouted out in Latin, *"Beatae Mariae Virginis Perdolentis, Haemolacria.* Tears of blood! She tells me to save the Jews." The monks were sceptical and came up the stairs to the pulpit. When they saw the bleeding tears, they got down on their knees and prayed. This infuriated Jonathan. "Stop praying, you fools, you have witnessed a miracle, and the message is clear. Run as fast as you can and stop the burning of the Jews. Jesus Christ was a Jew and those who burn them will burn in hell for eternity!" With that, the monks ran out of the cathedral so fast they were tripping over their habits. One of them turned round to look again at the monk on the pulpit and swore to his dying day that the man who rang the bell to alert them to St Mary's bloody tears evaporated before his eyes like the smoke from the pyres. No more Jews were burned at the stake in Portugal thereafter.

# Chapter 14

## Baruch Spinoza, 1656

A week later, Jonathan approached the house of Dr Adler, imagining what horrors he had for him this week and was pleasantly relieved by his welcome. First the young shaman asked after his patient's well-being. "Well, I've recovered from the psychic trauma you put me through last week. It was almost like you've cauterised a wound. I've had no panic attacks this week, and all my dreams as far as I can remember were pleasant and free of sinister door frames. I think your bizarre treatment is working."

"I'm pleased yet not surprised. This week your task should be enjoyable, merely reverting the reputation of one of greatest Jewish philosophers to his rightful place in the pantheon of scholars. The events occur about 150 years after the massacre of Lisbon but are linked to a family who escaped the *auto de fi* in Spain and Portugal, to a safe haven in the tolerant and liberal city of Amsterdam. His name of course is Baruch Spinoza, who is famous for being excommunicated rather than his genius as a logician. Baruch Spinoza was the son of Michael d'Espinoza, an importer of dried fruit and nuts from the Iberian Peninsula. Michael was a well-respected member of the Amsterdam Jewish community and acted as a *Parnas* (elder or representative) of the union of the three orthodox synagogues and a governor of the community's schools. Baruch rapidly showed his affinity for study, logic, and dialectics before he reached the age of fourteen when he left school to join his father's business. Although his formal education was over, he continued on his own volition to study the Torah and the Talmud. At a very early age he made known his 'heretical' views during open discourse amongst adult study groups. Even before publishing his first works, he was already in trouble by advocating his opinion that the Torah was not of divine origin, that Moses should command no more respect that Mohammad or Jesus of Nazareth. He also expounded his views that there was no afterlife of the soul. Even though he was only a callow youth, perhaps trying to provoke controversy and attention seeking, the community went incandescent with rage and on 27 July 1656 pronounced a *herem* (excommunication) on the young man. These are the exact words that were used." At this point Dr Adler picked up an ancient looking leather-bound tome and turned to page marked with a strip of paper and then read with sarcastic fastidiousness as follows.

*"By the decree of the Angels and by the command of the holy men, we excommunicate. Expel, curse and dam Baruch de Espinoza with the consent of God... cursed be he by day and cursed by he by night; cursed by he when he lies down and cursed by he when he rises up... The Lord shall not spare him, and the Lord shall blot out his name from under heaven. ... No one shall communicate with him in speech or writing nor accord him any favour nor stay under the same roof as him nor be within four cubits of his vicinity nor shall read any treatise composed or written by him."*

He then banged down the book on the table with meaningful and sincere fury. "And that's just a shortened version! It is difficult to understand the fierceness and bile of this decree making an outcast of a naive young contrarian before he had published a single word. His first work, *Treatise on the Emendation of the Intellect,* was written in about 1660, where he argues in favour of a worthwhile life rather than a pointless death. This beautiful line of prose in the treatise reads to me as an adumbration of all that was to follow.

*"But love towards a thing eternal and infinite feeds the mind wholly with joy and is itself unmingled with any*

*sadness wherefore it is greatly to be desired and sought after with all our strength.*

"Eventually Spinoza selected to exile himself to a nearby village rather than living in the toxic environment anywhere near the Amsterdam Jewish community. There, left in peace, he trained as a lens grinder and continued his studies and writings. It is something of a cliché to say that his lenses allowed him to see more clearly than his Jewish compatriots. It remains a mystery why this young man was subjected to a *herem* and such a vicious decree. Your task is to travel back 350 years to Amsterdam, track him down, find out why he thinks he was ostracized and then seek a meeting with the elders of the Jewish community to see if they can retract the *heren* and welcome him back into the fold. If you read his two important works, ethics and the treatise, you will understand my passion. He was certainly not an atheist and his interpretation of the Talmud on ethical behaviour and governance, if valued, might have avoided pogroms and wars over the next three centuries."

"I'm sorry," replied Jonathan. "That task must be impossible. This is not just saving an individual, but millions lost in the wars with all sorts of unintended consequences, such as overpopulation and famine."

"But Jonathan, as the Talmud says, *whosoever saves one life it's as if he saved the world.* Also remember the past, the present, and the future are not linear constructs but like the double helix that can split and rejoin with each other. Tiny errors in this process may be by chance beneficial, and this is what drives evolution.

"Timelines can also evolve. By chance the year 1656, the year of Spinoza's *heren* was the year Jews were allowed back into England under the governance of Oliver Cromwell. I want you to offer Spinoza to act as a disciple who will carry his master's teachings across the Channel to a more liberal environment that would be more supportive of his teachings. At the same time, I would entrust you with a tougher task and that is to persuade the elders of the Hebrew community to rescind the curse. I will delay your journey by a week so that you can read Spinoza's *Ethics* to win his trust. Here, borrow my copy and return it next week when I will transport you to seventeenth century Netherlands."

***

For the next seven days Jonathan buried himself into a translation of *The Ethics* kindly provided by Dr Adler. Perhaps drowned himself rather than buried himself would be more appropriate, as he had to keep coming up for air. He was a professor of philosophy who had read avidly since the age of seven, and at the age of eighteen had even read Popper's *Conjectures and Refutations* but *The Ethics*, although using the English translation, was almost unreadable. Nevertheless, after two or three attempts in a quiet room, in his most comfortable armchair and with a glass of eighteen-year-old Talisker in easy reach, the penny dropped. Here he was in the twenty-first century, a disciple of Karl Popper, someone steeped in the scientific school of falsifiability and hypothetico-deductivist logic, trying to make sense of the philosophical writings of a seventeenth century Dutchman proving his propositions using Euclidian inductive logic and deductive syllogisms that were promoted by Aristotle. He thought it might be a good idea to make notes so that he could write up this experience into a book for students, to help them understand the history of scientific and moral philosophy. What is a syllogism? *A syllogism is a form of reasoning in which a conclusion is drawn from two given or assumed propositions (premises); a common or middle term is present in the two premises and a conclusion.* That definition itself was difficult to understand so he wrote two examples:

1.  All men are mortal,
    Socrates is a man,

97

*ergo*. Socrates is mortal.

2.    Van Gogh was a great artist,

Van Gogh never sold a painting in his lifetime,

I'm an artist whose paintings never sell *ergo* I'm great.

The first makes sense but the second is nonsense.

The next problem was aggravated by the fact that Spinoza uses words like "substance", "attributes", and "essence" that must have had different meanings in seventeenth century philosophy from what we would understand today. Then there was the problem with the words inductive and deductive. Essentially inductive logic makes predictions from repeated observation to a generalised conclusion whilst deduction assumes that if certain premises are true then the conclusions are true. It wasn't until the insights of the eighteenth century Scottish philosopher, David Hume, that these ancient Greek concepts of logic where overturned. Ultimately the logic favoured by Spinoza was dismissed by Bertrand Russell's in his book *The History of Western Philosophy*, when he goes so far as to say "Aristotelian logic was a dead end followed by 2,000 years of stagnation… I conclude that the Aristotelian doctrines are wholly false, anyone in the present day who wishes to learn logic will be wasting his time."

In spite of all that, what Jonathan found remarkable was that when you leave out all the antiquated logic and just look at the conclusions for each test of the truth, Spinoza ends up pre-empting most of his deductions that emerge by applying modern scientific philosophy.

First of all, was he an atheist? Well clearly no, as the first half of *The Ethics* sets out to prove the existence of God. He applies thirty-seven propositions based on his axioms and concludes that there is a God if defined in his precise way. "Whatever is; is in God, and nothing can exist or be conceived without God."

So, what is beyond doubt is that Spinoza's achievement was to show man and his world as an inextricable unity, and man himself master and servant of the fate that creates him.

Spinoza defines God as a "substance consisting of infinite attributes, each of which expresses eternal and infinite essence". Translated into more familiar terms, God is not distinct from the world but identical with it. God is nature and nature is God and concludes:

*"In the foregoing I have explained the nature and properties of God. I have shown that he necessarily exists, that he is one: that all things are in God, and so depend on him, that without him they could neither exist nor be conceived."*

From this bedrock, following many steps of Aristotelian logic that Jonathan couldn't follow, Spinoza arrives at a definition of good and bad behaviour.

*"By good, I understand that which we certainly know to be useful to us; by bad, I understand that which we certainly know will prevent us from partaking of any good. The good life is that which is most favourable to our nature, the bad life which it is most opposed. Vice and wickedness are to be avoided, not because they are punished by God (who engages in no such absurd endeavours), but they are at variance with our nature and lead us to despair."*

In other words, virtue and evil are not rewarded or punished by God; virtue brings its own reward, and evil delivers its own punishment! Having reached the end of the book after six days' intense study and neglect of his family, Jonathan took a deep breath, laid back in his chair, sipped his scotch and smiled from ear to ear whilst thinking, "I love this man, he was certainly 350 years ahead of his time. I can't wait to meet him and make sure that his work will never be forgotten."

With all that knowledge under his belt, Jonathan felt well prepared to take on the bigots of the Jewish community in Amsterdam at the time of Baruch Spinoza's excommunication, but once he turned up at Dr Adler's door the following week, he learnt how his task had mutated. "I'm sorry, Jonathan, but during the time you've been studying Spinoza's *Ethics* the space/time worm hole for 1656 has closed, and it is too late to cancel the curse of the *heren*. In many ways this makes your task easier. I will teleport you to the nearest hole-in-the-wall that drops you into the Netherlands in 1661. You will land in Rijnsburg a small town just north of Leiden that is fifty kilometres south of Amsterdam. You will be surprised by what you see and all you need to do is to persuade Baruch to give a copy of his book written in Latin and then carry it across the channel to one of the *Cinque Ports* on the coast of southeast England and then find your way to Robert Hooke at the Royal Society in London. He was a friend of Spinoza, and the Royal Society was founded by a group of liberally minded and scientific gentlemen led by Sir Isaac Newton.

***

The next thing Professor Tannenbaum witnessed was a small sailing boat with a bright red sail, making its way under a double-beam drawbridge across a narrow canal, looking just like Van Gogh's painting of Arles. On the other side of the bridge was a single story, brick walled cottage with a green tiled steep sloping roof. A few other cottages and a church spire were scattered around on the neighbouring hillocks pretty against an azure, blue sky. He waited for the boat to pass under the bridge until the two beams dropped that allowed him to cross the water and knock on the cottage's door. The door was opened by a plump smiling man wearing a leather apron round his waist. He had a red bulbous nose and twinkly blue eyes and looked to be in his fifties. He wore large glasses with wire frames that magnified his eyes. He then started speaking Dutch that sounded like his was choking on fish bones, the first time Jonathan had encountered this problem. When it became obvious to the man at the door that the stranger couldn't understand a word he was saying, he switched to French, which acted as a common tongue. "Good morning, sir, I guess you are not Dutch, and we seldom have visitors from outside the Netherlands, where do you come from and how can I help you?"

"I come from London Town in England and was looking for the famous philosopher, Baruch Spinoza, who I'm told lives nearby," replied Jonathan.

"Well, you have come to the right house, although I assume you mean Benedict Spinoza, the famous lens grinder," laughed the man at the door. "My name is Herman Homan, a scientist and a surgeon, and Benedict is my best friend, who rents rooms at the extension at the back of my cottage. He has many enemies and likes to keep himself to himself, so before I take you in, I need to know who you are and what you want of him?"

"My name is Professor Jonathan Tannenbaum, professor of scientific and moral philosophy at London University. I am a great admirer of Baruch… sorry, Benedict Spinoza, and wish to introduce his work to my university."

"In which case you are very welcome, but before I take you round to his workshop, I must alert you that he no longer writes or speaks about philosophy and considers himself a humble grinder and polisher of lenses. Follow me." Dr Homan then led Jonathan through a cosy front parlour, through a scullery that looked as if it was also used as a chemical laboratory, overloaded with bottles of coloured powders, ceramic blue and white jars, and retort flasks. They then walked down a passage with red brick walls, at the end of which was a bright blue door. Dr Homan knocked at the door and shouted, "Bennie, you have an English professor come to visit. He looks harmless and claims he admires your work."

A voice from behind the door replied, "Tell him I can't take on any more customers, I've got too much on my bench."

"He is not interested in a pair of reading glasses or microscopes; he wants to talk to you about your work on philosophy!"

This was followed by a silence in the next-door room, and the noise of a chair scraping back, footsteps and a petulant, "Coming, coming." The man who opened the door was not the kind of man Jonathan was expecting. He looked older than his years, he wore a shabby gown that looked like a habit worn by a monk, his head was covered by an embroidered kippah, and he was covered from head to toe with a dust reflecting the light. Yet in spite of this, his big dark eyes retained their spark of intelligence and curiosity. He bowed to his guest and invited him in with a wave of his right arm. "Welcome, Professor, please excuse the dust, come take this chair."

The room had walls made of blocks of stone painted with white distemper with two large windows letting in the sunshine. The centre of the room was a large wooden structure that looked like a primitive lathe driven by a foot pedal. The most striking contents of the room were the shelves carrying complete or components for microscopes, telescopes, and humble eyeglasses. Everything reflected the sunlight through a miasma of dust. Jonathan started coughing and it was rapidly agreed by Homan and Spinoza that further conversation would be more comfortable conducted in the parlour at the front of the house. Jonathan began the conversation by introducing himself and the reason for his visit. "My name is Jonathan Tannenbaum; I'm a professor of the history of moral and scientific philosophy at University College London. From my name you may guess I am a Jew and it's worth noting that Jews have been welcomed in England since the time of Oliver Cromwell. I represent a small group of academics who have learnt of your teachings and are anxious to import volumes of your works to our more liberal colleges. I also act as an agent for Robert Hooke, one of the founders of the Royal Society, whose president is the famous Sir Isaac Newton. Hooke's most famous work was with the microscope. He published his observations in the celebrated *Micrographia*, which included spectacular enlargements of insects, plants, minerals, and household objects. He claims to owe you gratitude for the quality of the lenses you provided to help him build his microscope. We will pay whatever you wish, as your teachings are worth more than gold."

To which Spinoza replied, "My dear Professor Tannenbaum, I am flattered and deeply honoured by your visit and your kind words, but there is one hurdle that cannot be vaulted, and that is the fact that there are no books to be handed over. To understand this, listen very closely to what I say. I continue working on *Ethics* and have corresponded with scientists and philosophers throughout Europe. I've begun writing a theological-political treatise, which addresses theological and political issues such as the interpretation of scripture, the origins of the state, and the bounds of political and religious authority while arguing for a secular, democratic state. Meanwhile my very close friend, Adriaan Koerbagh, recently published a book that criticised organised religion, denied the divine authorship of the Bible, and asserted that miracles were impossible — ideas similar to those of mine. Since then, secular authorities have enforced the Reformed Church in Amsterdam's orders to ban the distribution of his so-called 'blasphemous book'. He died in prison. You can now understand why I'm too terrified to publish yet I'm desperate to disseminate my writings, not to achieve fame, but to help improve the lives of the common man."

At that point Jonathan thought that Mr Spinoza was close to tears. There was a silence in the room, with their heads bent down as if they were a congregation of three at prayer, until the silence was broken when Jonathan leapt up and proclaimed, "I've got it, by Jove I've got it. Give me your texts written in Latin, a language understood by all academics, and I will have them published anonymously by Cambridge University Press."

Spinoza nodded his agreement and quickly assembled copies of all his handwritten codices packed together in a parcel of hessian tied with string that created a cross with a loop at the centre to help Jonathan carry manuscripts to England. His journey across the channel, then finding Robert Hooke in London, is a story in itself. Sadly, Spinoza died of silicosis at the age of forty-four and never lived long enough to enjoy his fame and respect amongst the scholars of the western world.

# Chapter 15

## The Taking of Jerusalem and the Russian Civil War 1917

At his next visit Jonathan was taken aback when Dr Adler implied that he had no more to offer for the health and welfare of his patient. As it was, he was feeling better and had no more panic attacks, but what came next came as a surprise. "Dear Professor Tannenbaum, I now have a confession to make. Up until now my first concern was your mental health, but along the way I've achieved two other objectives. These were to protect your family lineage from your past to the future of the next two generations, and last but not least, ensure that the teaching of Benedict Spinoza were transported to the British Isles that will allow one of your grandsons to be inspired in a way that would secure a synergy of faith and science that will protect and multiply the children of Israel. But first we must draw your attention to the past of the matriarchal ancestry of this grandson. In other words, we must consider the birth of your wife, Shoshanna, in Jerusalem, in 1940, during the Second World War. But before that event we must go back to 1917, at the time the British army battelled with the army of the Ottoman Empire during first World War. The guns were still booming when General Sir Edmund Allenby rode down the Jaffa Road to the Jaffa Gate. The most famous city in the world, after centuries of strife and vain struggle, had fallen into the hands of the British Army after four hundred years under the control of the Ottoman Empire. The Foreign Office telegraphed Allenby to avoid any grandiosity. The general demounted and walked through the gate, accompanied by American, French, and Italian legates, and watched by all the patriarchs, rabbis, muftis, and consuls, to be greeted by the mayor of Jerusalem. Many wept for joy and strangers greeted and congratulated each other. Allenby was accompanied by Lawrence of Arabia, who had just survived the greatest trauma of his life. In late November, on a solitary recce behind enemy lines, he had been captured at Derra in Syria. Lawrence managed to escape, and Allenby summoned him just as Jerusalem fell. Lawrence gave up his Bedouin gear and borrowed a captain's uniform for the day. 'For me', he wrote, 'my appointment in the ceremony of the Jaffa Gate was the supreme moment of the war. The one which, for historical reasons, made a greater appeal than anything on earth.' Allenby climbed the steps to the platform to read his proclamation about 'Jerusalem the blessed', which was repeated in French, Arabic, Hebrew, Greek, Russian, and Italian, carefully not mentioning the word that was on everyone's mind: crusade. Finally, the mayor handed over the city keys, and Allenby marched through the gates and formally opened the great wooden doors to the Church of the Holy Sepulchre and invited in all the religious clerics of the many Christian sects. Allenby then placed Indian Muslim troops on guard at the Temple Mount.

Among the cafes near the Jaffa Gate, Arabs and Jews debated the future of Palestine. It was a huge breadth of opinions on both sides. On the Jewish side, this extended from the ultra-Orthodox who despised sacrilegious Zionism, by those who envisaged Jewish colonists fully integrated into an Arabic Middle East, to the extreme nationalist who wanted an armed Hebrew state ruling a submissive Arab minority. Arab opinion varied from nationalist fundamentalists, who wanted Jewish immigrants expelled, to democratic liberals have welcomed Jewish aid in building an Arab state. At this period of time, the geographical zone known as *Palestine* was delicately balanced between *'Palestinian Jews'* and *'Palestinian*

*Arabs'*. Whatever happened next would lead to the final outcome, the establishment of the state of Israel in 1948.

"Meanwhile whilst this was going on, the Russian Civil War had broken out and the link between that apocalypse and the birth of Shoshana in Jerusalem in 1940 is where you come in! Come now and take a walk along the Moyka embankment in St Petersburg in 1917. One last thing, please take these maps, one of the centres of the city and a second one of the eastern front lines in World War 1 in 1917, and this copy of a letter from Lord Balfour to Chaim Weizmann dated 1916. You will find them useful."

Once again Jonathan walked through the time-space membrane and once again he found himself in a space he had visited in the past on a lecture tour.

***

He was standing on the northern embankment of the rover Moyka close to the junction with the canal named the Griboyedon channel, looking south towards the monstrosity known as the "Church of our Saviour on the Spilled Blood". It had many onion-shaped domes and pinnacles all multicoloured. It looked more like a Disneyland palace than a church. As far as Jonathan's taste was concerned it was vulgar and over-the-top, yet it was a very important monument that marked a very important event. In 1881, Tsar Alexander II was stabbed to death by a terrorist, and his death was blamed on the Jews. Pogroms exploded all over Russia and tens of thousands were murdered.

At this point Jonathan knew where he was but had no idea what was needed of him to save the future of Shoshana's parents. He knew he had flown back in time 107 years, yet the architecture looked much the same as when he made a visit for a conference on the ethics of clinical trials, fifteen years ago. He thought he might see evidence of the time shift by the costumes worn by the pedestrians. He looked left and right along the embankment and was surprised to find it empty, but at the same time he heard noises from the west that sounded like the unruly crowd of football hooligans. Out of curiosity he followed the noise of the crowd walking along the loop of the Moyka that would take him in the direction of the winter palace. He reached the back of the crowd in no time, as it seemed to have filled the huge square in front of the palace and that had spread across the Nevsky Avenue and spilled over into to the gardens in front of the Baroque headquarters of the admiralty. Most of the crowd were working men in shabby old clothes and shapeless trousers. Others wore stained blue dungarees, and some were wearing jackets with brass buttons looking like veteran soldiers. Many wore caps like those favoured by Lenin. Nearly everyone carried a blunt weapon, pitchfork, or antique rifle. The noise rose to a crescendo, when suddenly there was the boom of several cannons and screaming was heard from the front of the riot. The crowd started backing and panic broke out when a huge body of cavalry came galloping through the centre, swiping left and right with their sabres leaving bleeding bodies trampled on the ground.

Jonathan didn't wait to see any more and ran for his life down Konnogvardeyskiy Bulvar in a southwest direction. When he could run no more, he collapsed behind a tree trunk and got out his map to see where he was and where on earth he should be making for. The map showed he was only three blocks away from the Grand Choral Synagogue on Lermontovskiy Prospket. He somehow sensed that it had been predetermined he should find his way to the epicentre of the Jewish community in St Petersburg, if only to find Shoshana's parents, whose maiden name was Polyakov. The synagogue was a huge melange of Moorish and Byzantine motifs with a green copper dome and alternate terracotta and yellow lateral rows of bricks. As it was not the Sabbath or one of the High Holy days, the grand interior was empty of a congregation, but he soon found the shammash, the Jewish beadle, who guided him to the office of the chief Rabbi Yitzchak Katzelenbogen.

As Jonathan entered the office, the rabbi looked up from a thick book he was reading, with raised bushy grey eyebrows that cast a shadow across his eyes. He wore a black skull cap that balanced on a hedgerow of unkempt grey hair that cascaded down the payot in front of his ears to link up with a moustache that covered his upper lip and continued halfway down his chest. In spite of that he had a kindly look, more curious about the unexpected stranger than anger at being interrupted in his studies. He opened the conversation with the multivalent verbal question mark, "Nuh?" followed in Yiddish that translated as, "Who might you be, stranger? I was not expecting anyone today and alerted my congregation to stay at home and lock their doors. The Cossacks are out attacking the revolutionary workers by the winter palace and that means their bloodlust will not be satisfied without another pogrom for the Jews."

To which Jonathan replied, also in perfect Yiddish, "My dear and honourable Rabbi Katzelenbogen, I'm well aware of that and witnessed it with my own eyes and that had me running to your great synagogue. I come as an emissary for Dr Chaim Weizmann, our leader in the Zionist movement. I come with good news at a time of despair.

"First, the British army have conquered Palestine and driven out the Ottoman Forces from Jerusalem. Furthermore, Lord Balfour has just been made foreign secretary and has written this letter to Dr Weizmann, with these words that I will translate into Yiddish. *'You have convinced me that history cannot be ignored, and that if a home was to be found for the Jewish people, homeless now for nineteen hundred years, it was vain to see it anywhere but in Palestine.'* I come to you with the responsibility of saving your community from further murderous pogroms and creating a fertile and religious renaissance in Jerusalem."

The rabbi took off his *pince nez*, held it up to the light and gave them a good polish, then turned to his visitor and with a touch of irony in his voice asked, "It might help if I knew your name, where you come from, and how in God's name you can help us?"

"Forgive me, Rabbi, I'm a nervous wreck having run all this way from the winter palace. I'm too old for this, I've just turned eighty-three! First my name is Jonathan Tannenbaum, I'm a Professor of Philosophy at London University, with three children and nine grandchildren, one of whom is training to be a rabbi. The reason I was chosen for this task would take too long to explain and my only credential is this copied letter from Chaim Weizmann."

To Jonathan's surprise the rabbi replied in English good enough to follow in spite of a guttural accent. "My dear Professor Tannenbaum, welcome to St Petersburg and the Grand Choral Synagogue. I'm familiar with the efforts of Chaim Weizmann, and like most of my congregation, I'm a Zionist. I am genuinely pessimistic about the future of the Jews in Russia now there is a civil war breaking out at the same time of the world war. We would welcome the Germans conquering Russia, as Red or White the Russians hate us. The poor Russians think we are all rich and the rich Russians think we are all Bolshevists. Furthermore, in spite of your country fighting Germany allied with Russia, we learn that England treats its Jews well, as you can confirm. I agree therefore with Dr Weizmann that in this barbaric maelstrom known as Europe, the safest place for Jews might be Palestine, where we can start rebuilding our indigenous nation, the state of Israel. So, Professor, how do you suggest I might transport my community to the promised land?"

"All I can offer you is the map of the front line in the war between nations. You would need to give this line a wide berth as the howitzers are shelling each other over distances of many kilometres. We must look at the map together, then with your knowledge of the Jewish communities in different lands, we could plot the route," Jonathan replied.

After a few minutes of contemplation, followed with a great smile that shone through the foliage of his hirsutism, the rabbi responded. "I will use the network of the Rabbani in the largest communities on the way, who might provide guidance and hospitality. We can make a start by sending a young *yeshiva bocher* across the front to alert the chief rabbi of Riga, which is close to the eastern front, who has the approval of the German High Command for rabbis to serve the local Jewish population, not just the German Jewish soldiers. He is a good friend of mine who will start off a network of Jewish communities along our route. Once he returns with a message of support, we can get moving. To begin with we have no chance of crossing the front line by land, but we can sail round its northern limit by sea. Many of my congregation are wealthy traders who own cargo ships, but on this occasion the cargo will be the whole Jewish community of St Petersburg. We will appear to be sailing to Helsinki but then turn southwest around the island of Dago, then turn south into the estuary of the river Daugava, which will take us to the heart of Riga. From there we will make our way due south towards Warsaw, then Budapest and onwards to the neutral countries of Sofia in Bulgaria and Salonika in Greece. From there we will take a ship to Haifa and from there complete our pilgrimage across the promised land to *Yerushalyim*, the City of Peace. The journey might take at least a year, and by then, please God, the war will be over! The children of Israel travelled 40 years in the wilderness to reach the promised land, so who's complaining?"

Jonathan could barely believe that this old man had such a remarkable brain to think so logically and with such rapidity. But then he remembered that debating the laws of the Talmud with other rabbis was a very good exercise for thinking quickly.

"Rabbi Katzelenbogen, I think you are a genius. When will you start planning this huge endeavour?"

"Well, right away. I will summon my messenger immediately and then call a meeting of the board of governors this evening." He then went to the door and called in his shamash. "Moishe, go get young Avram Polyakov from the yeshiva, and schlep him here as quickly as possible." He then turned took at his visitor and noticed his face had gone white.

"My dear friend you look like you've seen a ghost."

"Not a ghost, Rabbi, more like an adumbration of the future."

Jonathan acknowledged his task was done and that he would meet his Shoshana's father before he returned to London in 2024.

# Chapter 16

## The Rise and Fall of Eugenics and the Start of World War 2
## 1937–1941

The opening words of Dr Adler at Jonathan's next visit were so alarmist that the old philosopher broke out into a sweat as symptom of the overdrive of the sympathetic nervous system. "Professor Tannenbaum, your next campaign is to prevent the Germans from invading the United Kingdom and murdering the whole Jewish community, obviously your family included." He then held his hand up to delay Jonathan's exasperated response. "Just hear me out and then you'll understand. I'm sure you understand the 'butterfly effect'. This effect grants the power to cause a hurricane in China to a butterfly flapping its wings in New Mexico. It may take a very long time, but the connection is real. If the butterfly had not flapped its wings at just the right point in space and time, the hurricane would not have happened. A more rigorous way to express this is that small changes in the initial conditions lead to drastic changes in the results. You will act as the butterfly, and the chain reaction will take care of itself. Remember that if America had not joined the allies after the attack on Pearl Harbour on 11 December 1941, when in addition to declaring war on Japan they declared war on Germany, the Germans would have invaded the UK within months. We forget that the isolationists, led by the America First Committee, were a large, vocal, and powerful challenge to President Roosevelt's efforts to enter the war in Europe. Charles Lindbergh was perhaps the most famous isolationist. Charles Lindbergh of the dramatic transatlantic flight in *The Spirit of St. Louis,* as well as being a famous aviator, had also been a womaniser, eugenicist, anti-Semite, and an unrepentant admirer of Hitler and Nazism. At the same time there were famous eugenicists in the UK led by Francis Galton and his most prominent acolyte, Flinders Petrie. Flinders Petrie was a famous archaeologist or pioneer in the field of Egyptology. Whereas his close friend, Francis Galton, was the founder of the eugenic school of thought, and worked closely with him to provide skulls and long bones from his archaeological digs with the hope of corroborating the teachings of Galton. Petrie claimed that that there was a 'Dynastic Race', that was of pure Caucasian blood that entered Egypt from the south, conquered the "inferior" mixed race then inhabiting Egypt, and slowly introduced the finer dynastic civilisation as they interbred with the inferior indigenous people. 'Racial Photographs from the Egyptian Monuments' was the first work Petrie completed for Galton that provided a series of 190 photographs of the various races conquered or visited by the Egyptians. After this he continued working for the Galton Laboratory, collecting, measuring, and delivering skeletal remains. In fact, the laboratory requested so much from Petrie that, in 1895, there was no more room for the skulls and skeletons. As a result, the Anthropometric Lab was expanded. Petrie was also affiliated with a variety of far-right groups in England and was a dedicated believer in the superiority of the northern peoples over the Latinate and southern peoples. Petrie did not stop his eugenic mission there but presented ideas about social change that reflected deep-seated eugenic influence. In *Janus*, a book he published in 1907, he argued that if a state is successful, it is because a majority of its people, or at least a majority of the people who were in positions of power, were of good character. Thus, in order to create or maintain a society's integrity, the state must support the 'best stocks' and 'tax down the worst stocks' To achieve this vision of utopia it would be necessary to 'carefully segregate fine races and prohibit continued mixture, until they have a distinct type which will start a new civilisation when transplanted'. The segregation of 'fine' races would be done through state-monitored marriages and reproduction as well as state-monitored abstinence and sterilisation. He objected to reforms on child welfare that favoured nurture over nature as a way of overcoming poverty and low expectations of life. His most repugnant view was to dismiss the poor as being the 'worst stock' and the urban poor almost looked upon as separate race, using the expression 'weeding out inferior stock'. In short, this repulsive man was promoting an ideology that guided the barbaric application of racist theory by Adolf Hitler thirty years before he came to power. In the pre-war era, Petrie was head of the British Palestine Exploration Fund and had the authority to approve or disapprove the conduct and reporting of all the archaeological digs north-west Egypt all the way up to Syria. One of those digs was your old friend, Lachish. The head of that excavation was a modest young man, JL Starkey. Starkey was born in London, the son of a surveyor. As a child he was not much interested in formal education but spent much of his spare time reading about archaeology and visiting the British Museum. During World War I, he served in the Royal Air Force and at one time was posted to a lighthouse for some months on coastal reconnaissance, where he continued to read the books on archaeology that were sent to him. After the war he attended evening classes in Egyptology at University College, London, where he came in contact with Flinders Petrie and started studying Egyptian hieroglyphs. In 1926, Starkey joined Petrie as his first assistant at Tell Jammeh, near Gaza, applying his experience with workmen in Egypt to the newly engaged and untrained Bedouin. In 1932, Starkey left Petrie to lead his own expedition, financed by Sir Henry Wellcome. The chosen site was Tell el-Duweir, identified as Biblical

Lachish. In January 1938, at the age of forty-three, Starkey's career was tragically cut short. On 10 January, he was murdered by a party of armed Arabs on the track leading from Beit Jibrin to Hebron *en route* to the opening of the new Palestine Archaeological Museum in Jerusalem. Putting all the pieces together one might speculate that JL Starkey had made another extraordinary discovery at Lachish of such importance that if it challenged the very heart of eugenics at a time that Adolf Hitler was about to go to war and weed out the 'inferior stock' such as the Jews. Your role is to act like a detective and reopen the case of Starkey's murder. When you pass through the time-space membrane this time, you will recognise the landscape, but this time the year will be 1937. You will naturally be wearing khaki top and shorts and a hat with a wide brim to protect you from the harsh sun. Claim that you've been sent as a helper from the Palestine Exploration Fund, an expert in ancient Hebrew come to examine the 'letters'."

***

He arrived at the tentlike office that leant against the remains of an old Arab house at the time of the midday sun, when the whole team were resting in the shade and drinking cold water from a nearby well. They were surprised to see him, but a fresh face was welcome, and a kind-looking lady named Olga called Mr. Starkey over to meet the new member of the team. He was somewhat bewildered to welcome this stranger without notice; he blamed the postal service that had often failed them in this remote spot in the middle of nowhere. They shook hands and immediately took a liking to each other. He was found a camp bed in one of the freestanding tents in the archaeological little "village". That evening sitting round a campfire, they exchanged travelers' tales and even sang "campfire" songs that reminded Jonathan of his youth as a boy scout. He slept that night and awoke to the day when a remarkable

116

discovery was found by chance.

The "finds" were about 200 yards outside the protective walls at the northeast sector of the Tell.

The chance discovery had an element of drama combined with comedy. It was early evening just before supper, when a bunch of young boys from a nearby Arab village were kicking a ball around and one suddenly disappeared as if the earth had swallowed him. The others looked on in amazement until galvanized into action by terrified screams that seemed to come from below where they stood. On closer inspection it appeared that a sinkhole had opened under the feet of the unfortunate lad. As the others peered over the edge, they could just make out their teammate yelling his head off and begging them to save his life. Two of the older boys lay flat on their stomachs and gingerly wriggled to the edge of the grassy edge of the hole, reached in and grabbed one hand each and then pulled him out like a cork from a bottle. He was white with terror and kept gabbling on about dead bodies and skeletons. Once they had calmed him down, the two older boys looked over the edge again and could just about recognize what looked like a rib cage reflecting the oblique rays of the setting sun. Whilst the gang stood guard around the perimeter of the sinkhole, the leader of the pack ran off to summon one of the grown-ups from the expedition. As luck would have it, the first adult he encountered was Andrew Fleming. Andrew was a Scotsman studying osteology in the department of anatomy in the medical school at University College Hospital. He was carrying out fieldwork for his PhD in paleo-osteology as part of Starkey's team. So far, he had not much luck in finding human remains, but he had already collected sufficient material to deduce that the diet of the Ancient Israelites contained fish, sheep, goats, and beef. That was hardly surprising, so he assumed the boys had stumbled on the remains of an ancient abattoir that for reasons of hygiene and discretion had been built beyond the limits of the city walls. As night was falling, Andrew collected his flashlight and followed the boy back to the hole guarded by the other children. When he shone the beam into the pit, he confirmed that these were animal bones but that a more thorough examination would have to wait until the next morning. He gave the boy, who had inadvertently made the discovery, a shilling for his pains, who then skipped off happily to tell the tale of his terrifying experience to his family, in a nearby farm on a hillock due south of the Tell.

***

The following morning, after an early breakfast, Andrew Fleming accompanied by James Starkey and the newcomer, Jonathan, strolled along the meadow from their encampment to the pit containing the bones, followed by an excited gang of local young boys.

The young osteologist took out his trenching shovel and cleaned the turf around the hole in the subsoil until he came to the edge of the chalk rock that formed the roof of the pit. They were a bit disappointed to find that this was simply a burial pit for animal carcasses, rather than a built structure that might have represented an abattoir. Fleming extended a makeshift ladder down the pit, manipulating it through the pile of bones until it found a solid purchase on the floor of what appeared to be a cavity that had been carved out of the soft rock. The cavity extended outwards to form a bell-shaped cavern from the access portal, accidentally discovered by the hapless lad the previous evening. He then gingerly stepped into the cavern and made his way down to the top layer of skeletons. After a rather superficial examination he found something surprising and called up to Starkey above him, "I say, James, I found something very odd, let me pass up these bones so I can be sure of my initial guess." After a few moments sifting through the bones, he passed up a femur, half a pelvic bone and a near intact animal skull, to the waiting hands of his boss. He then

118

climbed back out of the hole and sat cross legged on the grass and examined the skeletal remains in the clear sunlight. "Any idea what these are, James?" Starkey shook his head, so Andrew continued, "These bones come from a pig, not part of a kosher diet for your ancient Hebrews, you'll agree. How old do you reckon this charnel house might be?"

"Well from what I've seen of the structure so far, it reminds me of the underground complexes we unearthed in Maresha a few years back and those certainly antedated the Hasmonean Kingdom by a long way," replied Starkey. "My guess is that it is a sixth century BC structure from before or around the time of the Babylonian conquest. Let's clear out the bones for you to log and examine properly and then see what clues we might find at the bottom of the pit below these carcasses."

Starkey, who by now had lost interest, went about his business leaving Andrew Fleming and Jonathan to carefully supervise the removal of the bones with the eager help of a band of local boys. They set up a trestle table and camp chairs at the edge of the pit and carefully logged and described each bone as it was passed up to them by the chain gang of cheeky young men who thought this was the most interesting day of their lives. For Andrew it was a rather tedious job after the original excitement, once he was sure that most bones were of porcine origin. Why this was the case could be debated with the other members of the expedition, over a gin and tonic at sundown that evening.

After the lunch break during the heat of the noonday sun, the osteologist and his helpers returned to work. By this time Fleming had estimated that he could account for about three hundred dead pigs by simply counting the remains of pelvic bones and skulls. Just before the anticipated afternoon tea break, a long bone was pocked out through the hole in the ground and carried over to Andrew, who took it from the boy barely giving it a glance, his eyes still on his notebooks.

Suddenly he recognized that the bone was significantly much heavier than anything else he'd handled that day. He turned his head to look at what he was holding in his left hand and noted with a start that it was the femur from a human skeleton. On closer looking he then noticed an iron arrowhead bedded in the shaft of the bone. His heart leapt with excitement, nearly pushing Jonathan over, and immediately dispatched one of his urchin helpmates to fetch the boss, James Starkey. Starkey arrived within minutes breathless with exertion having captured the excitement displayed by the little message boy. Fleming wordlessly handed him the femoral bone and Starkey whipped out his magnifying glass to study the arrowhead, muttering to himself, "Mm, mid-iron age, Mesopotamian design, near perfectly preserved by dry chalk cavern with narrow mouth, could only be Babylonian Empire period." Then turning to Fleming he continued, "Well Andrew, glad you joined us now? This bone almost certainly comes from a Judean defender of Lachish just before the taking of Jerusalem. You've got a gold mine here. If I'm correct this might be the burial ground for all the defenders of the city before the Babylonians overran it. I would guess the pig carcasses thrown on top of the Judean soldiers was meant as the final insult to their faith. Let's set up some floodlights powered by a generator to get a quick idea of the size of the task ahead. This find is too precious to barge in upon without careful planning."

Two hours later under the unforgiving brilliance of floodlights, James and Andrew cautiously stepped down a ladder in the cave that was anchored on the hard virgin rock deep below an ossuary of human remains that stretched as far as the eye could see. They were reluctant to test their weight on this cavern of dry bones but at least they could estimate the enormity of the task ahead.

They decided to organize a chain gang of the village children, with the smallest and lightest standing on the bones and passing them up to helpers at ground level. These would be divided into two teams, one selecting and organizing the human skeletal remains to be logged and later examined in detail by Fleming and the other to collect up any artefacts like arrowheads or bronze scales from a coat of mail. Olga was given the task of auditing the bones and Jonathan the role of auditing the iron artefacts. Any intact skulls were to be carefully preserved for detailed morphometric examination by James Starkey once the clearance was complete. These rare specimens would then be used to either corroborate or refute Flinders Petrie's theories of race.

On the face of it, Starkey's plans made good sense and once work restarted human remains went one way to Andrew and all other artefacts went the other way to Starkey to be classified and logged.

The bones piled up and were arranged logically into sets of right and left femora, tibia, clavicles, skulls and so on.

On the other table remnants of ancient armour, arrowheads, beads, and leather straps soon piled up. It took nearly three days to clear down to the virgin rock around the perimeter of the bell-shaped cavern before an extraordinary pyramid of about 100 human skulls was discovered. Witnessing this bizarre arrangement suggested that the first 100 Judean captives were killed by decapitation and their heads organized in a ritualistic manner before the bodies were dumped without ceremony on top. The final insult was then to bury the remains of hundreds of Judean captives under a layer of the carcasses of pigs.

Andrew and James estimated that the total number of skulls accounted for 1,500 brutally murdered defenders of Lachish, an adumbration of Stalin's massacre of Polish officers in Katyn in 1940.

The task at hand was huge and Starkey needed to increase his number of volunteers to carefully log and classify the artefacts on the one hand whilst logging and organizing the skeletons into the equivalent human units. Once again Jonathan's appearance was welcomed. Only once this repetitive work had been completed would he allow himself to start work on the treasure trove of human skulls. This resource would be the ultimate test of Petrie's predictions about race and cranial capacity. Unknown to Starkey, Flinders had been aware of this discovery a couple of days earlier from a spy in the team of local boys and was trying to contact the sponsors of the dig in London to allow him to take control of cataloguing the human remains. Telegrams had been sent but replies were yet not forthcoming.

The next afternoon Professor Petrie ambled on to the site of valley of dry bones as if only hearing of the discovery that morning. Starkey showed him around whilst Petrie exuded avuncular charm and complemented the team on their excellent work. Having inspected the crudely reconstructed human skeletons, early iron age arrowheads, and other such artefacts, he was then guided to the pit where he could look down on the pyramid of skulls that were left to last. He was clearly taken aback but refused the offer of a descent through the narrow aperture at the apex of the cavern, apologizing that his weight and girth might on one hand leave him stuck like a cork in a bottle or on the other hand destroy the rickety hand-built ladder leading down. Starkey found Petrie's good humour unnerving and completely out of character. That evening over dinner served by the light of a campfire, the great professor was introduced to Professor Tannenbaum, who had no recall of recruiting this stranger, but said no more. He then politely asked James Starkey if he might have a hand in the classification and intra-cranial measurements of the skulls. James' heart sank as he could think of no gracious way of refusing the professor's polite offer.

Either by divine intervention or a low-pressure system

drifting in from the Judean hills, a torrential storm hit the encampment that night. The burial pit flooded, and much damage was done to the excavations. They worked half the night bringing the new finds from the pit into the safety of the stone-built offices of the dig, but there was no question of continuing their work until the weather improved. Petrie went back to Gaza in a huff and renewed his efforts to try and get Starkey's sponsors to hand over the skulls for his safekeeping.

After the storm passed over, work restarted on the collection of skulls. They were each numbered with Indian ink on the frontal bone and measured with calipers along the classical diagonals of cranial morphometry. Each skull then had the cranial bones removed by a circular saw so that in cerebral volume could be estimated. Along the way Andrew came across three skulls bearing the stigma of trephination. In other words, holes had been drilled into the skull as a primitive act of surgery. Even more remarkable was the evidence that the victims had survived the procedure to fight another day. This was deduced by observing the cribriform fringe of new bone formation surrounding the edges of the circular defect.

From this point onwards Starkey, supported by Andrew Fleming, engaged in a furious battle of wills with Flinders Petrie via post and radio. James and Andrew demonstrated unequivocally that the skeletons belonged to the Judean soldiers and were therefore descendants of the ancient Israelites who had populated the fertile plains of the eastern Mediterranean coast. Yet against all the predictions of Petrie's theory of race, these bones belonged to a race with a cranial capacity equivalent to a modern day European of Caucasian lineage. Petrie couldn't accept this refutation of his precious theory. He couldn't challenge the morphometry of the skulls, as the team was using his methodology and instruments. He therefore argued that these soldiers could only be mercenaries from Sparta or ancient Greece.

Matters came to a head when out of the blue James Starkey was summoned to attend a meeting with Flinders Petrie in Berlin. They were to meet with Professor Eugen Fischer at the Kaiser Wilhem Institute of Anthropology, Human Heredity, and Eugenics, who was to provide a second opinion on the interpretation of Starkey's calculations. Apparently, Eugen Fischer had developed his own methods for designating race following measurement of the skull that was known as the Fischer-Saller scale. James thought that this was a complete farce because the man was a notorious racist who would only reinforce Petrie's prejudices. Strongly resenting the interruption of his fieldwork, James, accompanied with Jonathan, met up with Petrie at Atarot Airport near Jerusalem and from there flew to Cyprus and then caught BEA flight to Berlin.

The three men were met by Professor Fischer at Tempelhof airport and whisked off to Kaiser Wilhem Institute in the professor's huge Mercedes convertible. No sooner where they settled in Eugen Fischer's office than the professor was summoned to the telephone. He returned white faced and shaking. "Gentlemen," he said in a portentous voice, "The Führer has demanded an immediate audience. I briefed him about your visit, and he went into a tantrum over the suggestion that the skulls of ancient Israelites suggested a level of intelligence and cultural evolution that might match the Aryan race. Mr. Starkey, I advise you most sincerely to keep your mouth shut and leave the talking to Professor Petrie and me."

All that James Starkey remembered of that fateful meeting with Adolf Hitler, was the Führer screaming at them as he marched up and down in a petulant rage. Starkey to his credit refused to be bludgeoned into submission and considered himself lucky to have been allowed to leave without a quick visit to Gestapo HQ.

***

Despite that ugly row in Berlin, Starkey's work continued systematically once he was back on site. The more skulls that were examined, the stronger the evidence against eugenic theory of the Jews being low down in the league of racial intelligence was refuted. Eventually the statistical meta-analysis was complete, and Starkey thought it was time that these data were shared with the academic brotherhood around the world. Together with Andrew Fleming, they wrote a scientific paper, well-illustrated with diagram and photographs of example skulls, to be offered for publication to the Journal of the Palestinian Archaeology Fund (JPAF). To make sure it was delivered it was decided that he would deliver it via the central post office in Jerusalem. Andrew stayed behind to continue the work, but Jonathan volunteered to accompany him in the topless Willys Jeep. The vehicle was ideal for the rocky roads from Lachish to Ben Guvrin and the east towards Maresha and Hebron, before they could join the tarmacked main road north to Jerusalem. There was no doubt in Jonathan's mind that a spy amongst their team would have alerted one of the minions loyal to Flinders Petrie.

They set off at sunrise to avoid the midday sun with Starkey at the wheel and Jonathan in the passenger seat. They bumped along happily until they had to slow down to turn east at Ben Guvrin.

Suddenly there was a burst of gunfire coming from behind the rocks south of the road. Blood and fragments of skull from Starkey's cranium splattered Jonathan's face, and as he ducked down, he heard the hiss of missiles flying close above his head. Then everything went into slow motion. Starkey, by instinct, turned the steering wheel to the left before falling out of the Jeep dead. Jonathan grabbed the steering wheel to retain the vehicle on the road whilst it had some momentum, then jumped across to the driver's seat and slammed down his foot on the accelerator and escaped the murderous fusillade of bullets by the hairs on his head. Once he was out of harm's way, he turned around and had a quick glance of three men wearing chequered keffiyehs that covered their heads and faces. Jonathan, as well as being shocked, was feeling furious as he had no doubt who and why had planned this assassination and was determined to fulfil James Starkey's mission. He arrived at the walls of Jerusalem, looking gold in the brilliant sunshine, parked the Jeep and then asked the way to the central post office through the maze of lanes in the old city.

Fortunately, there were plenty of British soldiers to guide him, and Starkey's letter was posted.

The JPAF were quick to publish this seminal paper and acting as the flap of a butterfly's wing, racial eugenics was refuted, Charles Lindbergh and the isolationist movement were made to look idiotic, and America joined the allies in the war against Nazi Germany.

# Chapter 17

## The Holocaust and Jacob Tannenbaum
## 1942–1943

At his next visit, Jonathan found his interrogator more excited and verbose than previous weeks, and he soon found out why.

"Jonathan, you may remember at our first meeting that I suspected that sometime in the past, one of your ancestors, was guilty of a crime that had terrible consequences for other members of our race. I suggested that we would explore the past in hourly sessions to see if we can identify the point in time when this transgression occurred and see if you could

redeem your distant relative, by reversing the consequences of that misdemeanour. I think that time has come. This briefing will take a little longer than the previous sessions as you were only one year old at the time of the *Shoah* and would not have known what was going on at the time. Furthermore, when you were old enough to understand, your parents would have protected you from unsavoury facts concerning the Holocaust. Let me introduce you to Jewish *Kapos.* Jewish *Kapos* played a pivotal role in the history of the Holocaust. Imprisoned in concentration camps, *Kapos* were enemies and victims of the Nazis; they were Jewish inmates who were forced by the Nazis to serve as 'stand-in' guards. In effect, being a *Kapo* blurred the lines between collaborator, perpetrator, and victim. It was a ravaged landscape in which Jews, fighting for survival, faced many moral-ethical dilemmas and 'choiceless choices'. Heinrich Himmler, the Reichsführer of the SS, spoke bluntly about *Kapos.* In his speech to the generals of the German Army on 21 June 1944, he praised the *Kapo* system and emphasised its significance and success. Recruiting and deploying an army of *Kapos* was a cost-saving measure. Only a small number of SS men was required to oversee an ever-increasing camp population. Also, it drove a wedge between inmates, turning groups against groups and victims against victims. The strategy of 'divide and rule' paid off. What had been initiated in pre-war concentration camps was practised in ghettos following the outbreak of World War II; members of the 'Judenräte', Jewish councils, Jewish policemen, and agents of the Gestapo were forced to assist the Germans in implementing the programme of the Final Solution.

"*Kapos* were officially classified as 'prisoner functionaries', taking over supervisory positions within the so-called 'prisoner self-administration' of the camps. First and foremost, they were in charge of 'Arbeitskommandos', which were labour details that were deployed outside the camp. They also controlled the work of inmates within the camp barracks – in kitchens, laundries, sick bays, storerooms, offices, and other facilities. Around four million men, women, and children passed through concentration camps, of which about 10 percent might have assisted the SS in running the camps. In early January 1945, over 700,000 Jews and non-Jews were still alive in concentration camps, among them perhaps 70,000 *Kapos*. Most of them survived the war. With few exceptions, they were never held accountable for the services they had rendered. *Kapos* were rewarded for their work. They were granted privileges. They received better food, clothing, and housing. Wearing a distinct armband displaying their status, they were spared hard labour and harsh treatment. They enjoyed better hygienic conditions, which in turn offered a layer of protection against rampant diseases. *Kapos* had easier access to flourishing black-market activities and corrupt dealings. Most importantly, power and privileges promised a chance of survival, provided they fulfilled the expectations of their SS masters. If they were caught out or unable to perform their duties, they were dismissed, punished, and henceforth treated as ordinary prisoners. Himmler told his sycophants: *'A Kapo gets special privileges. The minute we are not satisfied with him he stops being a Kapo and goes back to sleeping with others. He knows only too well that they will kill him on the first night.'*

"It was a catch twenty-two. Your grandfather, Jacob, was a *Kapo,* and your role is to protect his death from the Nazis or death from his fellow Jews in the death camp, Treblinka!" At this point Jonathan ran out of tolerance and blew his top. "Dr Adler, how can you know this? It's a load of rubbish. Are you taking me as a buffoon? You might be a devout practitioner of hocus pocus Kabbalah, but you can't know better than me the life of my beloved grandfather. In 1933 Hitler became chancellor in Germany riding on the tide of anti-Semitism. As things got worse and worse for the Jews in the neighbouring country, my parents, and grandparents, anticipated that it would spill over into Warsaw, and my grandparents emigrated to the UK in 1937, two years before the invasion of the Nazis. How can you know better than me?"

"Cool down, my friend, I do know better than you and here is why," replied Dr Adler. "There is nothing magic or kabbalistic about this knowledge, you could find it yourself. You were born in 1940, and your parents never told you the truth, nor were you curious when you reached the age of enlightenment. My source comes from the details recorded by the Nazis about all their Jewish captive that were discovered at the time the concentration camps were liberated. All those data are recorded in the museum of Yad Vashem in Jerusalem, which have now been digitised and are available online. It's true that your family came to England in 1937, but your grandfather returned to Warsaw on business matters in August 1939 just before the German army walked into Poland and occupied the land. In 1940, all the Jews in Warsaw were rounded up and forced into a walled-off ghetto. At its height, as many as 460,000 Jews were imprisoned there, in an area of 1.3 square miles, with an average of nine persons per room. With Nazi cynicism, they were left to govern themselves and your grandfather was appointed to the Jewish council of elders, with authority over the Jewish police. Your grandfather survived the revolt in 1943 and joined the 50,000 survivors who were transported in cattle trucks to Treblinka. This is where you come in."

***

Professor Tannenbaum suddenly found himself crushed together with about forty men and women in an open-top truck, possibly used for carrying sheep to the abattoir. Some of these innocent Jews in the squash were probably making the same journey. A tall, handsome, middle-aged man was also struggling to find a comfortable place to last for a fifty-mile journey. When settled he turned to Jonathan and said, "Hello, old man, I don't think we've met before, what's your name?"

Jonathan had to control his laughter being described as an old man by his grandfather before responding. "My name is Jonathan Tannenbaum, and I used to teach philosophy at the university."

"That is a remarkable coincidence, my name in Jacob Tannenbaum," his grandfather replied. "We must be related. Where did you live before you were caged in the ghetto?"

"I escaped from Lvov ghetto a month ago only to be captured by the Gestapo and schlepped to the Warsaw ghetto a couple of days ago," replied Jonathan.

"Well, Uncle Tannenbaum you must be one of my second cousins, even though our surname is quite common," his grandfather replied. "I think it is my duty to look after you. You see this arm band on my left arm, if you look carefully, it has a small Magen-David and the letters K-A-P-O, *Kapo*. It means I'm in charge of this bin full of Jews and try to avoid trouble by following our master's commands. It is a sickening responsibility but one of the only ways of surviving. Stick close to me and do as I say, otherwise you will end up in the extermination camp." He refused to explain anymore and remained tight lipped until they arrived at the end of the railway track at the Treblinka concentration camp.

Once they had stopped at the long platform, where about fifty of Nazi SS soldiers awaited them, the unloading of the passengers was rapid and brutal. Suitcases were thrown onto a heap never to be seen again, and a selection process was made by three of the senior officers, the young and fit sent to the left and the rest to the right. When it came to their turn, Jacob Tannenbaum wearing his *Kapo* arm band was directed left and as the SS officer was about to direct Jonathan to the right, his grandfather intervened and swore that his companion was a skilled bricklayer. That for some reason made the SS officer redirect Jonathan to the left.

Once they were being marched to their destination and out of earshot of the guards, Jacob whispered the explanation. "Jonathan, you need to understand what's going on here. Treblinka is divided into two units. Those who were directed to the right will be taken to the extermination camp and within twenty-four hours will be murdered in a gas chamber. We have the honour of joining the forced labour camp, for the disposal of the victims. We are known as *sonderkommanda*. We have to cut wood to fuel the pits of the mass graves for open air pyres. In addition, we are mining for gravel and helping to build extensions of the gas chambers and crematoria, as they can't keep up the workload demanded by the Führer.

"That's why I claimed you were a bricklayer. Don't worry, it's more likely you will starve to death before they find out you are *not* a skilled bricklayer." The walk to their camp took about thirty minutes and any laggards were knocked on the head by the butt of one of their guard's rifle. Any that fell to the floor were shot dead and kicked aside for getting in the way of the march. Eventually they arrived at their barracks. There were about fifty long single level wooden huts capped with sloping corrugated iron roofs. Each were numbered on the door with white paint. Each side of their hut was full, from floor to ceiling, with three levels of shelves bearing straw filled paillasses. The only heat came from a wood burning stove in the centre of the aisle. Each hut was governed by a *Kapo*. Once the hut was full and the entrance door locked by one of the SS troopers, Jacob called for order and all the prisoners gathered round him near the stove. His words chilled them to the core.

"My name is Jacob Tannenbaum, and I am your *Kapo*. Look upon me as the Hillel sandwich you eat during the Seder night on the eve of *Pesach*. The Hillel sandwich is made of two squares of *matza* with *maror* the bitter herbs as the filling of the sandwich. You, the prisoners of the Nazis, are as brittle as *matza* but, like it or not, I'm what holds you together. I will make sure that you all obey the orders come down to us via the SS soldiers guarding each hut, these come down from *Sturmbannfuher* Theodor van Eupen, commandant of the camp who follows the orders of *Reichsführer* Heinrich Himmler. I am the bottom of the chain of command, and if I fail in my duties, I will be sent to the gas chambers. But I want to persuade you that it's in your enlightened interest that you obey my orders."

At that point one of the newcomers, a youth aged about sixteen, raised his hand like a schoolchild asking his teacher. "Please, sir, what is a gas chamber?"

For once Jacob Tannenbaum was at a loss for words. He was rescued when the door of the hut was thrown open and in stepped the camp commandant and two of his SS officers, looking splendid in their smart uniforms, horse-riding breeches, black high leather boots, and peaked caps bearing the skull head insignia of the SS. One of van Eupen's minions screamed, "Stand to attention," and all obeyed. The commandant then drew up a scroll of printed paper from one of his patched pockets, and with a sardonic voice made his announcement. "You Jews know what the ten commandments are and post them above the ark in your synagogues. Well, you can forget them under my supervision, I'm now your lord and this scroll carries a new set of ten commandments. Unlike your archaic list, this new decalogue describes the punishment you can expect if you break any of these laws.

1.    Thou shall have no other God but the Reichsführer.
2.    Thou shall not be idle.
3.    Thou shall not take the name of Adolf Hitler in vain.
4.    Forget the Sabbath day as thou shalt be working seven days a week.
5.    Honour your *Kapo* and your *Sturmbannfuher*.
6.    Thou shall not attempt to murder your guards.
7.    Thou shall not commit buggery.
8.    Thou shalt not steal food or wood for your stove.
9.    Thou shall not bear false witness against other prisoners.
10.   When in doubt think again.

The punishment for transgression of these laws will be fifty lashes, or if I feel like it a bullet in the back of your heads. That's enough for one day, we will turn off the lights as soon as you have jumped into your beds, and you will be counted and inspected at roll calls in the parade ground outside at 4.30 am tomorrow morning. Remember this is a transit camp on the way to your final destination as farmhands in the fertile region north of Vilnius. " He then nodded to his guards, who set about urging their captives into their bunks with the points of their bayonets.

***

Jonathan couldn't sleep, so at some unearthly hour he slipped out of his bunk and tiptoed towards the door where

133

Jacob, their *Kapo,* had the privilege of a camp bed for himself. He knelt down and whispered in his grandfather's ear, "Jacob, this is not a transit camp to anywhere but the gas chambers."

Jacob was not asleep and with a sharp tongue responded, "Do you think I'm a fool, Jonathan? Of course, the Treblinka camp has been built for the extermination of the Jews. Once we know the daily routine, we can think of the way we might escape."

***

The day began at 4 am when prisoners were awoken in their barracks by a guard banging an iron saucepan. The prisoners then given thirty minutes to use the toilet, get washed and get dressed, make their beds, clean the barracks, and have their breakfast, a shallow tin bowl of gruel. Toilet and washing facilities were only dirty water with no soap or toilet paper, shared by up to 2,000 prisoners. Anyone who completed these tasks too slowly faced lashes from a whip. This role was taken by a different caste of *Kapo* whose uniform bore a black triangle, that they later learnt were criminals who traded their time in prison for the sadistic pleasure of beating up the prisoners bearing six-point yellow stars over their heart. The prisoners were then lined up for the morning roll call, a registration of all prisoners in the camp, including those who had died in the night or those that were ill, on the *Appellplatz.* The prisoners would be counted twice, and any discrepancies meant that they were recounted. This meant that the morning roll call could take hours. Throughout this time, prisoners would have to stand outside whatever the weather. Any prisoners that collapsed or were found to be missing faced beatings, torture, or execution. On this their first day, the prisoners were stripped of their own civilian clothing and forced to wear a uniform that was patterned with blue stripes, although this wasn't always the case. The men were given a cap, trousers, and jacket to wear. Women wore a dress or skirt with a jacket and kerchief for their head. Some uniforms, for the higher-ranking prisoners such as *Kapos,* had pockets, which were extremely useful for concealing extra rations or having useful luxuries such as spoons or cutlery. On their feet, prisoners wore wooden or leather clogs. Socks were not supplied, and as a result many prisoners suffered with sores from rubbing. They then lined up again to have their registration numbers tattooed on their right forearm. There were three specialist *Kapos* trained as tattooists, and as there were 1,000 or more inmates, by the time their work was finished, they had to join another queue for their evening meal of black bread and thin vegetable soup. After that it was bedtime and lights out at 2100 hours. Throughout their first day Jonathan and Jacob Tannenbaum kept their eyes upon for the smallest detail that might suggest a flaw in the system that might be exploited for an escape. None were found but they remained optimistic that the daily routine might expose a defect in their cage.

***

Once roll call was finished the next morning and the sun rose, the prisoners set off for work. The occupants of Tannenbaum's hut were scheduled to cut wood to the furnaces of the crematoria fed by the gas chambers in Treblinka Two. The journey to the nearest forest was about five kilometres away was taken on feet wearing clogs. Despite the sheer exhaustion that many felt after malnourishment and fatiguing routines, keeping up with the speed of the march was essential. Those that fell behind were subject to severe punishment and torture. At noon, the prisoners were forced to march back for a noon roll call, and to collect their lunch of black bread. Work finished at 6 pm that day, and the prisoners were marched back to the camp to participate in evening roll call. Two inmates from another hut had died during the day but were also brought out to the roll call to be counted. After the evening roll call was completed, they were all sent back to their barracks, where

135

they had 'free time'. Most of the Tannenbaum's confreres were exhausted and simply retired to their beds, but for Jonathan and Jacob, this was the time to share their observations before 21.00, when lights were switched off and the prisoners were expected to sleep.

Jacob started the confab, "First, the best chance of escape is whilst we are working in the forest. I've noticed three things that might be of value. First, we were marching northeast having witnessed the rising and setting of the sun. Next the ratio of *Kapos* to Nazi soldiers is about five to one, and finally the Nazi soldiers are considered of no value at the west front. They all look forty or more and most are overweight and seemed to be as exhausted as us after the march to the forest. Anything to add, Jonathan?"

"Well yes, Jacob, something very weird. Each soldier is accompanied with an Alsatian dog on a lead. By chance I stepped on the foot of one of these dogs, who yelped, and instead of going for my throat, his ears went back, tail between his legs and backed his way behind his handler. The dog seemed frightened of me. To test this out I bent down to pat the head of another dog on the other side of the march, and the same thing happened. Alsatian dogs treat me like a ghost and are terrified by me. Perhaps it's my smell?"

Jacob went very quiet and chewed his lips in intense concentration, then decided. "Our choice is to die slowly or die quickly, the buggers are to exterminate all of us Jews one way or the other. So, we've nothing to lose. We just make it simple. Once we get to the forest the soldiers all sit down on one of the logs we've cut down, smoke a fag, or eat a sandwich. I'll choose the fattest of the soldiers and get him into a conversation as one of the trusted collaborators. You will make your way towards us slowly with your blanket wrapped around your body under your jacket. Once I nod you will pull out your blanket and start dragging it along the ground, I will crack the skull of the Nazi with a heavy branch of wood and together start running in the northeast direction. If your notion is correct, the dogs will not follow our trail, and we can only pray that other *Kapos* follow our example or at least intervene as the other guards figure out what has happened and reach for their rifles."

Jonathan suddenly realised this was the moment to fulfil his obligation defined by Dr Adler, and replied, "No, Jacob, that would be self-indulgent, we must use this plan to rescue as many of our co-religious prisoners who are scheduled for the gas chambers today, so we must run southwest to Treblinka Two to start a riot."

..........................

And so it came to pass that Jacob and Jonathan escaped from Treblinka followed by 200 other prisoners who rioted at the same time on the way to the gas chambers. Several were shot dead, but many lived on, running northeast across the Soviet war front to join the Rd Army of the USSR and play their part in the victory over the Nazi aggressors. One of those who escaped was Marek Edelman, who was born in 1922 in Warsaw. When the occupation of Warsaw began in the fall of 1939, he got a job as a courier at the Bersohn and Bauman Children's Hospital in Warsaw. In November 1940, the area of the city where he lived became part of the Warsaw ghetto. For some time, due to his work at the hospital, he had a pass authorising him to walk outside the ghetto. In 1942 he was among the founders of the Jewish Combat Organization – a conspiratorial armed resistance movement of Polish Jews. He was one of the leaders of the Warsaw Ghetto Uprising of 1943. After the war, he settled permanently in Lodz, where he pursued his career as a renowned cardiologist. In 1998 he received the highest decoration in Poland – the Order of the White Eagle. He died in 2009, aged eighty-seven. He is buried at the Jewish cemetery at Okopowa street in Warsaw.

# Chapter 18

## Jonathan Tannenbaum Faces the Future Alone

Once Jonathan returned to his natural time-space niche, he reappeared in his bedroom with his wife shaking him awake. "Wake up, darling, it's 9.30 Sunday morning and we promised to go walking the dogs on the heath with Rachel and Helen. Have you had bad dreams? You've been shouting in your sleep." Rubbing the sleep from his eyes and slightly bewildered, he replied, "Yes, I had a run of nightmares, but I can't remember what they were." That was only a half truth. Much of what he experienced in this long sleep would define his outlook for the rest of his life. "Give me thirty minutes to use the toilet, get washed, get dressed and make the bed."

"You never make the bed, Jonathan, in your life," replied Shoshana, "but I'll give you thirty minutes to wash and shave and put on your casual cloths and walking boots."

Jonathan obeyed his instructions like an automaton, still bewildered to wake up at home, when in the past he had always returned to his time-space niche in Dr Adler's consulting room. Nevertheless, he felt refreshed and looked forward to walking across the heath extension with his daughters and their dogs, Bobbie and Luna. The day followed the usual pattern for a pleasant late spring morning, with the walk breaking for lunch of fish and chips at the Spaniards Inn with a pint of best bitter beer to wash it down. In the afternoon he spent a few hours working on his memoires, a game of bridge in the evening with their best friends, and early to bed at 10 pm. The next day he went to see Dr Adler with the good news that he was cured of his panic attacks and no longer experienced the sinister recurring dreams. He turned up as usual, rang the doorbell that suddenly reminded him it was nearly a year since he first visited the Kabbalist, and he was going to celebrate his eighty-fourth birthday the following week. The door was opened by a distinguished middle-aged man wearing all the garbs of an ultra-orthodox rabbi. Jonathan greeted the man at the door, "Good morning, Rabbi, I take it you must be Dr Adler Senior back from New York, I have an appointment with your son."

The man at the door with a quizzical look responded. "I think you might have the wrong house. I *am* a Dr Adler Senior, but there is no Dr Adler Junior in this house. Neither have I come back from New York, although I hope to go there one day. I hope there will be a rabbi Dr Adler Junior in the future, but at the moment I don't want him disturbed as he is practising for his bar mitzvah."

Jonathan felt giddy as he heard chanting from upstairs the haftorah for the parsha *Shelach l'cha*. The opening line was repeated, *vayishloch Yehashua ben Nun, min-hashitim shniim anoshem* (And Joshua the son of Nun sent two men out of Shittim to spy secretly). The very same of the parsha of his own bar mitzvah celebrated twice. Clearly there had been a significant error in the fine tuning of his space–time coordinates. Jonathan apologised for disturbing this Dr Adler and went home to think it through by himself.

......................

"I have learnt my lessons from the past, and have been cured of my anxiety state, I'm therefore left to myself to plan my future at a time of resurgent anti-Semitism, *autres temps, autres moeurs*. I consider myself a lucky man having lived with good health to the age of eighty-four. Although born in 1940 I have no memory of the war or even the austerity after the war. My earliest memories were whingeing when the ration books denied me an endless supply of sweets. I've had an excellent education; primary school, grammar school, and university all paid for by the state. I've enjoyed my academic work as a professor at the

LSE and never needed to deny my Judaism. I've never experienced anti-Semitism, neither have my children, but sadly my grandchildren are growing up in a new cultural medium that is starting to favour a new pandemic of that toxic virus. Middle East politics is a minefield both literally and figuratively and I would dearly like to stay out of it and enjoy a happy retirement, writing my books. Sadly, even if I try to disengage, the ripples of the Arab Israeli conflict lap at my doorstep. We have recently finished celebrating the eight days of the Passover. Our suburban synagogue looked like the 'Green Zone' at the border of Afghanistan, with barriers outside to protect us from car bombs and security guards at all road junctions within a square mile radius. We were even warned against congregating in the synagogue courtyard after service for our traditional gossip in case we made too attractive a target. No, it's not the fascist British National Party that worries our community, but the threat of Islamic fanatics. You may think that I exaggerate or that our community is paranoid, yet we are acting under the advice of the metropolitan police. In addition, a close friend of mine who is a judge at the Old Bailey told me about a recent case where three young British-born Islamic zealots, where sent down for three years for possessing material linked to the manufacture of suicide bombs along with inflammatory anti-Semitic literature that included reprints of *Protocols of the Elders of Zion*. Furthermore, you don't have to look far to see the reality of the threat. Across the channel our French co-religionists have faced the reality of Islamicist terror, with murder of orthodox Jews and firebombing of synagogues. As an indication of what French Jews are suffering at the hands of the North African Muslim extremists, the largest group of immigrants to Israel now happens to be the middle-class French men and women. But worst of all are the Saturday marches of thousands made up of Islamicist provocateurs, aided and abetted by useful idiots, chanting 'From the river to the sea,

Palestine will be free', without knowing which river and sea they are referring to. They carry the Palestinian flag and placards carrying the outrageous fabrications that Israel is an apartheid state and guilty of genocide. The rebirth of the blood libel. This outbreak of virulent anti-Semitism was triggered by the events following the incursion of Palestinian terrorists into southwest Israel at the time of a music festival on 7 October 2023, killing 1,200 innocent civilians and dragging away over 250 Israelis as hostages. Every epoch in history has come up with its own brand of anti-Semitism, that hydra headed monster. In its turn this anti-Semitism left to its own devices, has led to attempts at genocide."

*'The Egyptians did evil to us-as it says: Let us deal with them wisely and, if we happen to be at war, they may join our enemies and fight against us and then leave the country.'*

"That quotation comes from the *Pesach Haggadah,* the book that provides the order of service for the *Seder* service on the eve of Passover. This quotation probably represents the first anti-Semitic rationale to justify Jewish persecution. The ancient Egyptian rationale for persecution of the Jews might be judged as kind of adumbration of the accusation of dual loyalties, even though the Jewish tradition has always been fierce loyalty to the ruling classes of the host country. In the British United Synagogue, we pray for the health and welfare of the royal family every Sabbath before the Torah scroll is returned to the arc, so it was with the time of kaisers and the tsars.

Following this proclamation the ancient Egyptians set up concentration camps and forced the Jews into slave labour. However much of the subsequent story is historical truth or myth, is of little relevance, but it is worth pointing out that when we recite the story of the ten plagues, we spill a little wine to remember the suffering of the innocent victims of God's wrath. Also, each year for the last two millennia, at the end of the *Seder* service, we sing the verse, *'l'shana ha'bah b'Yerushalyim'* (Next year may we return to Jerusalem)"

"The suffering of the Jews under the Roman yoke is well described in Josephus' *The Jewish Wars*. This led to the sacking of the second temple in 70 AD, the dispersal of the Israelites to the four corners of the Roman Empire, with 100,000 sent as slave labour to the Hispania, the Iberian Peninsula. That population ultimately gave rise to the Sephardic community. The last stand of the Jewish refugees after the sacking of Jerusalem was at Masada overlooking the Dead Sea. The siege ended in 74 AD following mass suicide of the defenders."

"In 135 AD, Hadrian's victory in bar Kokhba's revolt resulted in 580,000 Jews killed: effectively a genocide of the Jewish population at that time. The Romans renamed the new territory Syria Palaestina to complete the disassociation with Judaea. Jerusalem was re-established as the Roman military colony of Aelia Capitoline and an unsuccessful attempt was made to prevent Jews from living there. Many Jews left the country altogether for the diaspora communities, and large numbers of prisoners of war are sold as slaves throughout the Roman Empire. After the fall of the Roman Empire, the land of Palestinia was controlled in sequence by the Byzantine Empire, 330–638 AD, the Arab Caliphate 638–1099 AD, and the crusaders 1099–1244. I grew up as a schoolboy with picture books of gallant knights in chainmail armour sporting a white doublet carrying a red cross. In fact, they were a bunch of hoodlums with much in common with the BNP who to this day sport the red cross of St George. They marauded across Europe looking for Jewish communities to wipe out with their blood lust whipped up by the blood libel promoted by their Christian clergy. This ancient libel, which is enjoying a reincarnation in the Palestinian school curriculum today, would have you believe that an essential component of the *matza* (unleavened bread) that we consume at the time of Passover, is the blood of a Christian (or maybe Muslim) child."

"The Jews in the Iberian Peninsula enjoyed a golden age during the time of the Caliphate, but things went pear shaped when the Christians took charge. The inquisition wasn't just concerned about Christian heresy; it wouldn't tolerate Judaism at all. Those Jews who refused to convert were tortured and there were many examples of mass murder. Burning synagogues with the Jews locked inside provided the murderers with an economy of scale that was admired and emulated by the pogroms in Eastern Europe in the last century. Eventually in 1492 all the Jews were expelled from Portugal and Spain to establish the Sephardi Diaspora. The fact that these refugees had lived there for close on 500 years was of no consequence and I have yet to hear a complaint on their treatment by the *Independent* or *Guardian*. Fortunately, they have done rather well after their dispersion, so who's to complain?"

"Jumping now to the nineteenth century we should in passing acknowledge the institutionalized anti-Semitism in France as exposed by the Dreyfus Affair that incidentally led to the creation of modern Zionism. I'm sure you're aware of the fact that a newspaper reporter at the trial was Theodore Herzl. In 1894, Captain Alfred Dreyfus, a Jewish officer in the French army, was unjustly accused of treason, mainly because of the prevailing anti-Semitic atmosphere. Herzl witnessed mobs shouting 'Death to the Jews' in France, the home of the French Revolution, and resolved that there was only one solution: the mass immigration of Jews to a land that they could call their own. Herzl concluded that anti-Semitism was a stable and immutable factor in human society, which assimilation did not solve. He mulled over the idea of Jewish sovereignty and published *Der Judenstaat* (The Jewish State) in 1896. In parallel with events in France, although far more deadly, were the Czarist Russian pogroms. These exercises in piecemeal genocide were fueled by the next perennial libel, the forgery entitled *The Protocols of the Elders of Zion*. The history of this vile fabrication, that was the excuse for the murder tens of thousands of Jews. Although accepted throughout the civilized world as a forgery, it has been reinstated for its value in promoting the Palestinian cause in certain Middle Eastern states."

"The Nazi German mechanized mass murder campaign was the most successful attempt at genocide to date known as the Holocaust or Shoa. It is still fresh in the memory of my generation, although considered ancient history to my grandchildren's generation. But again, it's worth remembering that Hitler's rhetoric fell on ground fertilized by the four apocalyptic libels, dual loyalty, blood libel, Deicide, and conspiracy theory. I was once shown round the cathedral in Freiberg. The guide pointed out a stained-glass window and apologetically pointed out the German legacy of anti-Semitism as permanently imprinted in the medieval coloured glass. The central figure was a beautiful blonde lady wearing a crown and riding a white horse. She represented Christianity. She was leading a donkey on a rope with an ugly hunch-backed man with a pointed hat sitting on the beast but facing its tail end. This of course represented Judaism. Around this central panel was a strip cartoon or graphic novel that could recount a tale for the illiterate congregants. It presented a beautifully detailed recipe to produce the Passover *matza* including the essential ingredient, the blood of a Christian child."

"Post Second World War we had the Soviet show trials and the 'doctors' conspiracy' that lead to tens of thousands of Jews joining the legions of slave labourers in the gulags. The 'Protocols' once again served their purpose. Ultimately, after massive global pressure and a courageous stand by the *refuseniks*, there was a second exodus to the promised land. I won't dwell too long on the pan-Arab persecution and expulsion of about 700,000 Jews in 1947–48. The *Mizrachi* Jews in Iran and Iraq could trace their history way back to the time of the Babylonian civilization in Mesopotamia. They again prospered in their diaspora and spent little time banged up in refugee camps, finding succor amongst their co-religionists around the world."

"Pan-Arab anti-Semitism has deep roots; however, Palestinian anti-Semitism is in a class of its own. During the Second World War, the leader of the Palestinian Arabs, the Mufti Haj Amin al-Husseini, was in exile in Berlin. The mufti called Hitler the 'protector of Islam' and supported the 'the final solution' as a handy way of getting rid of the Jews from Palestine. He also raised a military unit, 'Free Arabia', to fight alongside the Nazis and support Rommel's advance from North Africa. Modern day Palestinian anti-Semitism appears under two guises, the traditional dehumanization/blood libel/ protocols/Holocaust denial catechism, and a truly original high technology 'You-Tube generation' version, known affectionately as 'Pallywood' productions. Let me refer to some choice examples. In one of these charming videos, you will see a sweet little three-year-old Palestinian girl, who can already recite the teaching of the prophet that all Jews are apes and pigs. Other examples for grown-ups feature all the well-known Jewish stereotypes."

"I have seen many such examples, but I came over nauseous during my search for the best example of this hate mongering. It was produced like a soap opera portraying the usual suspects murdering a Palestinian child for his blood in preparation for the Passover matza."

"As far as the *Protocols of the Elders of Zion*, I'm sad to report it is still in print and available in an Islamic book shop near you. Over time the use of the *Protocols* in the Muslim world has become increasingly bold: they are published in and sold in bookstores, taught in schools, serialized in official newspapers accompanied by *Stuermer*-style cartoons, quoted on numerous sites on the internet, acted as a way to disseminate them to hundreds of millions of Muslims.

"The final weapon in the modern Palestinian anti-Semitism armamentarium involves the making of fraudulent video films to implicate Israel and the IDF in atrocities where innocent women and children are killed by mistake by Palestinian ordinance, used as human shields or caught up in the crossfire in a military skirmish. The most notorious of these was the tragic shooting of a young Palestinian lad, Mohmmad Al-Durah, at a crossroad.

"To understand modern anti-Semitism, you first need to understand the old style as described above. But for those who genuinely feel the need to understand the latest mutation of this virus, read on. It is gut churning, how a dangerous, worldwide coalition of Islamic terrorists, well-intentioned but profoundly misinformed students, right-wing fascists, left-wing ideologues, pious academics, opportunist European politicians and sensation seeking international media, have joined together to blame the Jews and the Jewish state once again for the current world crisis. Today's activism against the Jews often takes the form of anti-Zionism. Osama Bin Laden blamed the 9/11 World Trade Center attack on the US government's support for Israel. Since then, hundreds of synagogues have been burned, cemeteries vandalized, Jews threatened, boycotted, beaten, and killed. Turkish television has now started broadcasting a vehemently anti-Israel series entitled *Farewell,* which depicts actors dressed as Israeli troops shooting Palestinian children at point blank range, killing a baby after its mother goes into labour at a checkpoint, and lining up captured men in front of a firing squad.

"Iran enjoys a remarkable reputation in today's world, first in denying the last Holocaust and secondly in promising the next. God help us if they develop their own atomic bomb although the American air force recently knocked out their supply of Uranium 238.

In the meantime, Iran's ambitions in the Middle East, aided and abetted by its two client terrorist groups, Hamas, and Hezbollah, are not only the greatest threats to Israel but also the peace and stability of the whole world. Unquestioning support of Hamas and the hurrah for Hezbollah adds fuel to the flames, as judged by the flags flown openly in the great pro-Palestinian marches in central London."

"During the years since Israel withdrew from Gaza in September 2005, Hamas brutally replaced *Mahmoud Abbas*'s regime, the people of southern Israel were bombarded with 10,000 rockets. This was a provocation that no other country would have tolerated for so long and not once did the UN complain. Since the founding of the state of Israel in 1948, this tiny sliver of land, less than the size of Wales, has been provoked into four wars and countless skirmishes with unfriendly neighbours on all sides, not in the name of expansion but to protect its borders. After the 1948 war it wasn't Israel that annexed Palestinian land, but Jordan who occupied the West Bank, drove the large Jewish population out of East Jerusalem, destroyed their ancient synagogues, and later, in 'Black September', massacred many innocent Palestinian refugees. It was only after Israel invaded the West Bank after the Six Day War has that territory been demarcated as Palestinian. Indeed, the last 'legitimate' rulers of that land were the British, under the mandate that ended in 1947!

"Israel can only afford to lose one war, as its western border is the Mediterranean and there's nowhere else for a retreat. Most of the time the world looks on passively at these provocations and only becomes outraged when Israel retaliates.

"For a start it is essential to understand the centrality of the state of Israel in the mindset of both religious and secular Jews throughout the world. Israel is central to our sense of identity, our culture, and our faith. You notice that I leave out 'race' from that definition of identity because that is a rather vague term open to much misinterpretation (even carrying the threat of being labelled a racist), yet in one sense we are a race or a people if you prefer, as many of us possess a molecular genealogy that dates back to the Biblical time of the Israelites. This 4,000-year-old story explains why most Jews in the diaspora yearn for Zion and consider Israel their second home. Israel and the Temple Mount are as central to Judaism as the Vatican and St Peter's is to the Catholics."

# Epilogue

As an epilogue, let me return to outbreak of virulent anti-Semitism that was triggered by the events following the incursion of Palestinian terrorists into southwest Israel at the time of a music festival on 7 October 2023, killing 1,200 innocent civilians and dragging away over 250 Israelis as hostages. October 7th was the largest pogrom perpetrated against the Jews since the Holocaust. And yet within hours of news of the massacre being broadcast worldwide, and long before Israel had launched its current military operation inside Gaza, there was growing evidence of a remarkable phenomenon. Not the expected sympathy and solidarity with the Jewish people as they faced another enemy committed to their extermination. No. Quite the opposite, blaming of the victims. A campaign of hate directed not just against the Jewish state but Jewish people everywhere. Since then, the virus has only spread, and a new pandemic of anti-Semitism has grown exponentially.

Visitors to a mosque promoting inter-faith dialogue told they were not welcome because they were Jewish. The family who found their baby's passport defaced because they were Jewish. Apart from a list of individual alarms, and along with these incidents, an increasingly clamorous, and explicit, demonstrations of anti-Semitism on our streets during protest marches that included Swastikas, Hamas banners, and portrayals of Jews as exploiters, devils, and child killing pigs. Jews were frightened to get near these demonstrations or to wear any indicator of their faith. This was aggravated by the fact that many of these demonstrations were taking place near synagogues on the Shabbat, when men normally walk home wearing black hats carrying under their arm, their *tallis* in a soft bag carrying a gold embraided star of David. Their womenfolk are also conspicuous, wearing their finery often with a silver chain around her neck bearing a Magen-David star. History tells us that the dismantling of the right of Jews to live, like others, on their own terms' leads, inevitably, to the destruction of Jewish lives. It's an unyielding law of history that countries which are descending into decadence are those which are becoming more and more unsafe for Jewish individuals and the Jewish community – the Spain of the Inquisition, the Vienna of the 1900s, Germany in the thirties, Russia in the last decade. So, when Jewish people are under threat, all our freedoms are threatened. The safety of the Jewish community is the canary in the mine. These protests may ostensibly be presented as against Israel's actions in Gaza but in reality, they are directed against Israel's continued existence. The calls for boycotts, divestment and sanctions from protestors are endorsements of a campaign – the Boycott, Divestment, and Sanctions (BDS) campaign – which I can see is explicitly anti-Semitic. There were no BDS campaigns directed against Bashar Assad's Syria, the regime guilty of killing more Muslims in living memory than any other. There are no student encampments urging university administrators to cut all ties with China given what is happening in Xinjiang or Hong Kong, or what happened in Tibet. I know of no efforts to organise marchers in their thousands to demand immediate action to stop the persecution of the Rohingya or Karen people by Myanmar's government. A child might whinge, "It's not fair, Daddy", but I'm a grandfather and feel a sense of responsibility for my grandchildren. But what can I do, aged eighty-four, tired and dispirited? I have no fortune to leave to an Israeli charity and no connections to our leaders in parliament. But I've just membered the words of Dr Nathan Adler. My youngest grandson, Benjamin, has the knowledge, wisdom, and links between faith and science, to carry the flaming baton to continue the fight for truth whilst my fire shrinks to a sooty pyramid of flickering sparks.

# CODA
## 25 Years in the future

The Templeton prize is presented annually to a living person who has made an exceptional contribution to affirming life's spiritual dimension, whether through insight, discovery, or practical works. The prize for 2050 was awarded to Professor Benjamin Tannenbaum and was worth $2 million. Below is a copy of his acceptance speech.

......................

First of all, I must acknowledge my beloved grandfather, the late Professor Jonathan Tannenbaum, he sent me on this journey to achieve this award. This point of time in my life is worth the *shehecheyanu* prayer. *Baruch atah, Adonai Eloheinu, Melech haolam, shehecheyanu, v'kiy'manu, v'higiyanu laz'man hazeh.* Blessed are You, Adonai our God, Sovereign of all, who has kept us alive, sustained us, and brought us to this season.

Next, I must acknowledge Michel de Montaigne's essays that I've read from cover to cover more than once and learnt from his writings that a life of reflection, thinking through moral dilemmas and rationalizing empirical observations, helps creativity and is good for peace of mind. Montaigne invented the mode of writing we now describe by the word *essay* derives from the French infinitive *essayer*, "to try" or "to attempt". In other words, to put on trial. I've never forgotten what a delight it was to read, as if the author was speaking directly to you over the passage of more than four centuries. His charm lies in the use of the first person throughout and the avoidance of the passive tense. He is even self-deprecating for his apparent egotism and tongue in cheek, claims that no one else has the expertise to compete with him in writing about himself.

Here is a passage where he warns the reader against accepting received wisdom.

*The tutor should make his pupil sift everything and take nothing into his head on simple authority or trust. Aristotle's principles must no more be principles with him than those of the Stoics or the Epicureans. Let their various opinions be put before him; he will choose between them if he can, if not he will remain in doubt. Only fools are certain and immovable.*

In other words, faith is no virtue, but uncertainty is! Then later, in a chapter headed Repentance, he writes:

*There is indeed a certain sense of gratification when we do a good deed that gives us inward satisfaction, and a generous pride that accompanies a good conscience...*

*These testimonies of a good conscience are pleasant; and such natural pleasure is very beneficial to us; it is the only payment that can never fail.*

Yet again, a great thinker argues that virtue carries its own reward. What a lovely man he must have been. The others in my list of philosophers that have influenced my thinking include Sir Thomas Browne, Baruch Spinoza, Voltaire, Immanuel Kant, Sir Karl Popper, and Roger Scruton. My own work, as you know has been to study the good, the bad, and the ugly of monotheistic religions, as well as atheistic ideologies. The direction of my research can be summed up by this quotation from *Monty Python's Life of Brian.*

*All right, but apart from the sanitation, the medicine, education, wine, public order, irrigation, roads, a freshwater system, and public health, what have the Romans ever done for us?*

To which I would respond with the most important decree in Leviticus:

*Thou shalt love thy neighbour as thyself. Leviticus 19:18*

I must remind us of all that whatever race, religion, or culture we come from, the simple command to love one's neighbour as ourselves is the bedrock of civilization. In response to this command, we should ask ourselves two simple questions, a) how do we best express our love? And b) who do we consider to be our neighbour? If one loves oneself then what single most important gift would you grant yourself? Ask anyone this question and they most always reply, the gift of good health. Therefore, if you love others then the gift you want for them is also good health. These others who you should love in an unconditional way are your parents, your spouse, your children, and grandchildren. I might then go on to joke that I hate my neighbours, that that is of course taking the words of the Bible too literally. To whom does this duty or commandment to love to extend? How wide is this circle of love? The immediate family, the extended family, our village, our tribe, or our nation state? The answer to this is simple. With globalization of commerce, social network information technology and relative ease of travel, the concept of the global village has matured and with this the duty of care from those countries that are resource rich to those countries that are resource poor becomes an ethical imperative. If we love our neighbours as ourselves, then we cannot stand by and watch them suffer nor must we squander scarce resources for tiny incremental improvements in health care for the rich whilst the poor of this world die prematurely from easily preventable or treatable disease. There are only two meaningful outcome measures in the evaluation of health care simply put; they are length of life (LOL) and quality of life (QOL). All other outcomes are surrogate and however compelling the results screening, blood tests, and medical images might be, they may not translate into improvements in LOL and QOL. LOL is of course easy to measure but QOL is not that easy to measure, but psychometric instruments for this purpose have been a focus in my research, quoting the words of Lord Kelvin, who described the first and second laws of thermodynamics. 'To measure is to know. If you cannot measure it, you cannot improve it.'

Does religion improve quality of life? The answer to this rhetorical question might be – *could do better*. Belief in heaven and hell, teaching of sexual guilt, denial of sexual orientation, promotion of celibacy as a virtue, anti-abortion and contraception, and misogyny do little to improve QOL. Religious leaders are beholden to exhibit a degree of humility, accept that what they preach might do harm, and do their best to improve the quality of life of their congregation. Let's start with heaven and hell. You cannot legislate against such beliefs, but you can at least temper the way they impact on QOL. The clergy should teach that virtue is its own reward and that to be virtuous in this life for the benefit of life after death in five-star accommodation is not a virtue but merely succumbing to bribery and that is a sin. The same applies to the concept of hell. Avoiding the temptation to covet thy neighbour's wife so as not to spend an eternity in a furnace stoked by demons is not a virtue, such behaviour never ends up well in any case. Furthermore, throughout history there was never any evidence that preaching fire and brimstone reduced the crime rate. I would go a little further, that should a religious leader preach this despicable load of garbage in front of vulnerable children, he or she should be reported to the appropriate secular authorities.

Celibacy is not a virtue but a punishment for a crime not committed.

*And God blessed Noah and his sons and said to them, "Go forth, be fruitful and multiply, and fill the earth".* Genesis 9:1

If you believe this is the word of God, then please note what God *didn't* say by way of a qualifying clause. There was no codicil to the effect that the act of multiplication should on no account be pleasurable, punishable by an additional term in the sin bin. The very fact that sexual intercourse is one of the greatest joys of life, bettered only by a good run down a black run on the *piste* on a sunny day in the Alps, accounts for its evolutionary advantage. The caste of high priests around the world should cease and desist from threatening their flock with fire and brimstone should they find pleasure in "recreational" sex with a consenting partner. This doesn't mean that promiscuity is endorsed, such behaviour carries its own penalty and should be included in the school curriculum as sex education.

The etiology of sexual orientation is complex and currently open to debate. Whether it's nature or nurture or a bit of each has yet to be resolved, but all agree that it is out of one's control and therefore should no longer be considered as a crime for prosecution in secular courts or as a sin for prosecution in the heavenly courts. The suffering of millions of young men and women over the last 2,000 years can only be imagined. I have little doubt that the acceptance of the LGBT+ community in recent years has enhanced their QOL scores that must have been at the lowest extreme in the era dominated by religious bigots and bullies. Of course, there are many benighted countries in the world today who deal with the LGBT+ community by throwing them from a roof top. In this way not only has their QOL been impaired, but their LOL has been shortened. This is murder and those guilty should be put on trial in some international court of justice. Finally, I wish to consider the three issues, anti-abortion, contraception, and misogyny, under the same heading. By these means women are denied their rights of self-determination. Why should we continue to accept the right of elderly, celibate, bigoted men, to bully women of all ages in their fertile years and deny the women their right to determine when and how many times they should give birth. Again, sex education in schools should take on the role of advising against promiscuity and the hazards of young teen-age pregnancies. Let the clergy preach about the virtue of love; their role in determining the birth rate is long past. I am glad to note the increasing role of women in high office in the Church of England and in many of the Jewish communities around the world. Once female clergy balance male clergy in positions of authority in all religious communities, the problem would be solved, but we still have a long way to go.

I concede that many of my most provocative recommendations above will have angered religious leaders in the spectrum "centre-right to extreme right wing", yet I am very sensitive to the fact that I might have offended many dear friends and family members who don't share my views. For them I offer a gamble, the flip side of Pascal's wager, because it excludes those who believe that this life on earth is merely a preparation for the life to come. Let us put our conflicting ideas to the test by conducting a trial or natural experiment. Let us take a large sample from our population that will include believers and non-believers. The believers would be stratified by their religious affiliations, and all stratified by demography (age, sex, country of birth, social class, etc.). Let us then study this cohort by offering psychometric QOL instruments, that include new psychometric instruments that have been developed that include 'spirituality' in the equation including the Daily Spiritual Experience Scale (DSES).

I will start off by testing myself on the DSES scale that covers spiritual domains such as awe, gratitude, mercy, sense of connection with the transcendent, and compassionate love. There are sixteen items on the scale that are scored from left to right, *many times a day, every day, most days, some days, occasionally, never*. I assume that the nearer your tick is to the left hand extreme the better the score (*many times a day* scores six and *never* scores 1) Using this system I score 53 out of a possible 96. I got top marks for the following items: *I am spiritually touched by the beauty of creation, I feel thankful for my blessings, I feel a selfless caring for others, I accept others even when they do things I think are wrong.* Of course, this is self-assessment, but I tried to be honest with myself otherwise I would have done better than a measly 55 percent.

God bless you all, and for those who don't believe in God, may you be touched by the beauty of evolution and the loveliness of the Milky Way!


.................

# Author's Notes.

In the years 1963–64, having just passed the first set of exams for a Fellowship at the Royal College of Surgery (FRCS) in London, I chose work as a second assistant in the department of surgery at the hospital in Afula in northern Israel to prepare myself for the final FRCS. In the spring of 1963, I was seconded to work as a medical officer at the excavations on Masada led by the Professor of Archaeology at the Hebrew University in Jerusalem, Professor Yigael Yadin. As well as running an accident and emergency clinic I was required to captain a team of volunteers working in the spaces between the double curtain walls along the edges of the east of the massif, facing the Dead Sea. The spaces between the walls were critical to an understanding of how the families of the Zealots lived. Amongst the rubble we discovered a stove with the remains of fish bones from their last meals, a hidden bag of copper coins and an almost intact glass perfume bottles that reflected the colours of the rainbow. Having read the Flavius Josephus' book, *The Jewish War* in preparation for the dig, I sensed that I was touching artefacts that had been touched by the hands of my ancestors, 2,000 years ago in the past. This was one of the most seminal events in my life, and I caught the bug of Biblical archaeology. I joined the Palestine Exploration Fund (PEF) with offices in London and visited most of the important archaeological sites in Israel. I carried out some original research about the digs at Lachish from the archives of the PEF and was asked to read and review a new book about Flinders Petrie and the history of eugenics. Even though I was a surgeon, I studied psychiatry and developed psychometric tests to measure the levels of anxiety and depression, amongst patients diagnosed with cancer. I was brought up in a conventional orthodox community but knew nothing about Kabbalah until I read the book, *Mystical*

*Kabbalah: The Tree of Life and Beyond* by Dr T Stephens. I chose the name Tannenbaum for my protagonist, not because of my surname, but for the mystical beauty of a coniferous tree. Baruch Spinoza is a hero of mine, I studied his works at a course in our local University of the Third Age (U3A), and reading a delightful book by Steven Nadler, *A Book Forged in Hell*. The story of 200 prisoners escaping the gas chambers at Treblinka is a fact but of course the involvement of a man called Tannenbaum is pure fiction.

Finaly, just as we were ready to print, I learnt that time-travel was first described in the *Talmud* from my Rabbi, Niki Liss, in Highgate Synagogue on the Sunday morning between the Jewish New Year and Yom Kippur 2025. The version of the Talmud he referred to was compiled by scholars in Babylonia, is the one most widely studied today. Its final redaction took place between the 3rd and 6th centuries CE. Generations of rabbinic debated about law, ethics, and Bible, structured as commentary amongst its pages to this day. The passage can be found in chapter *Menachos* on page 29b[2]:

*When Moses ascended on High, he found the Holy One, Blessed be He, sitting and tying crowns on the letters of the Torah. Moses said before God: Master of the Universe, who is preventing You from giving the Torah without these additions? God said to him: There is a man who is destined to be born after several generations, and Akiva ben Yosef is his name; he is destined to derive from each and every thorn of these crowns mounds upon mounds of halakhot. It is for his sake that the crowns must be added to the letters of the Torah. Moses said before God: Master of the Universe, show him to me. God said to him: Return behind you. Moses went and sat at the end of the eighth row in Rabbi Akiva's study hall and did not understand what they were saying. Moses' strength waned, as he thought his Torah knowledge was deficient. When Rabbi Akiva arrived at the discussion of one matter, his students said to him: My teacher, from where do you derive this? Rabbi Akiva said to them: It is a halakha transmitted to Moses from Sinai. When Moses heard this, his mind was put at ease, as this too was part of the Torah that he was to receive.*

Rabbi Akiva's dates are generally accepted as approximately 40/50 CE to 135 CE. He was a leading Jewish sage and scholar of the late 1st and early 2nd centuries who was martyred by the Romans in the aftermath of the Bar Kokhba revolt. Whereas Moses crossed the Nile (Reed Sea) in about 1250 BCE. This was time travel of more than a thousand years!